MAUREEN CHILD

ONE LITTLE SECRET

HARLEQUIN
DESIRE

HARLEQUIN®
DESIRE™

Recycling programs
for this product may
not exist in your area.

ISBN-13: 978-1-335-73535-5

One Little Secret

Copyright © 2021 by Maureen Child

This edition published by arrangement with Harlequin Books S.A.

For questions and comments about the quality of this book, please contact us at CustomerService@Harlequin.com.

Harlequin Enterprises ULC
22 Adelaide St. West, 41st Floor
Toronto, Ontario M5H 4E3, Canada
www.Harlequin.com

Printed in U.S.A.

Maureen Child writes for the Harlequin Desire line and can't imagine a better job. A seven-time finalist for the prestigious Romance Writers of America RITA® Award, Maureen is the author of more than one hundred romance novels. Her books regularly appear on bestseller lists and have won several awards, including a Prism Award, a National Readers' Choice Award, a Colorado Romance Writers Award of Excellence and a Golden Quill Award. She is a native Californian but has recently moved to the mountains of Utah.

Books by Maureen Child

Harlequin Desire

Red Hot Rancher
Jet Set Confessions
Temptation at Christmas
Six Nights of Seduction

Dynasties: The Carey Center

The Ex Upstairs
Ways to Win an Ex
The Wrong Mr. Right
One Little Secret

Visit her Author Profile page at Harlequin.com, or maureenchild.com, for more titles.

You can also find Maureen Child on Facebook, along with other Harlequin Desire authors, at Facebook.com/harlequindesireauthors!

My first book was dedicated to my husband, Mark, and now this one, too, goes to the man who first believed in me, supported me and loved me always.

I miss the hugs, the laughter, the midnight chats and the road trips. I miss knowing that you're just in the next room. I even miss the whistling that used to drive me nuts. And I'm blessed to have had you for so many years.

I hope the fishing is great where you are, honey. Save me a seat. I'll get there eventually. I love you.

One

Justin Carey looked around the conference room and told himself *this* was why he usually skipped family meetings.

He'd been sitting at the Carey Corporation for a half hour already and they were no closer to ending the meeting than they had been at the beginning. Maintaining the Carey legacy required a family meeting at least once a month and Justin avoided them as often as he could. Not that he didn't want to spend time with his family. But he definitely wasn't interested in becoming a link in the Carey family chain.

The Carey Center, basically a palace to the performing arts, was the grand dame in their holdings. But there were also five star restaurants and an upscale shopping center called FireWood and dozens of real estate holdings and none of it interested Justin.

He wanted to make his own way. Build his own contributions to the Carey legacy. And he'd felt as if he might suffocate if he'd fallen into line and taken an office here at the "mother ship."

Still, he had to admit that the last few months had brought changes. His sisters, Amanda and Serena, couldn't seem to talk about anything other than their upcoming weddings. And the oldest Carey sibling, Bennett, seemed almost...*relaxed*. Which was just unnerving.

Bennett had always been the most driven of them all. He ran his life on schedules and lists—and yet, since he'd sat down for the meeting that morning, the man had had a small, self-satisfied smile etched on his face. Leaning back in the black leather chair at the head of the table, Bennett watched the family like a benevolent old uncle. Amazing, Justin told himself, what finding love with Hannah Yates, contractor extraordinaire, had done for Bennett.

While he waited for the meeting to get going again after a short break, he watched his sisters. Amanda and Serena had their heads together over a bridal magazine, flipping madly through the pages, with the occasional sigh or muffled shriek of approval.

Only his parents' relationship hadn't changed. What he and his siblings were calling the Retirement Wars were still in full swing. His father, Martin, had promised his wife that when Bennett took over the Carey Corporation, Martin would retire and the two of them would do all the things they had talked about. But that time had come and gone, and Martin still couldn't let go. So Justin's mother, Candace, had moved out of their house and into Bennett's.

Justin smiled to himself remembering how hard Bennett had worked to get his mother out of his home—unsuccessfully. Though now that Hannah had moved in, too, Bennett didn't seem to mind as much. Just one more perplexing change among the rest. Hell, maybe he should attend more meetings. It might be the only way to keep up.

"Candy," Martin Carey said, "it's time this is over. We've got two daughters getting married, Hannah's moved into Bennett's house and they probably want some privacy…"

"Don't bring me into this," Bennett said.

Justin kept quiet and watched the byplay.

"Candy, you come on home and we can talk about the retirement plan."

Candace tapped one finger against the tabletop and shook her head until her short, chestnut hair swung at her jaw. "No, Marty. I'm not coming home now. I'm comfortable at Bennett's house. As a matter of fact, Hannah and I are having a wonderful time turning that beige palace into a home."

"Hey…" Bennett broke in again and now even Justin's sisters looked up, listening.

"I'm sorry, dear," Candace said with a wave of her hand. "But you know it's true. And Hannah is so talented at bringing homes back to life."

Bennett sighed and scowled.

"The kitchen is being redone as we speak and the living room has already been painted a wonderful, dark forest green…"

"I don't care what you're doing to Bennett's house," Martin grumbled.

"Well, you should. It's just lovely."

"Candy, I miss you," Martin said, gritting his teeth. "It's time you came back to me. Talk to me."

"We've done all the talking we're going to do already," Candace said softly. "You know what has to happen if you want this to end."

Justin winced on behalf of his father. He knew how much his parents loved each other, but he also knew his mother wouldn't give up if she thought she was right. His father had to know that, too.

"You're being unreasonable," Martin said.

"And you broke your word to me."

He looked insulted. "I did not."

"I'm sorry," Candace said, glancing around the room. "Are we on a cruise ship right now and I just missed it?"

Martin ground his teeth together and Justin wanted to tell his father to simply surrender. Candace Carey always found a way to win. None of her four children had ever been able to get around her, and her husband wouldn't have any luck with it, either.

While the family talked over and to each other, Justin sat back in his chair and looked at the room as an outsider. Because basically, that was just what he was.

In a world of tailored suits and high expectations, Justin was an Armani black leather jacket and charting his own course. He didn't take orders well, and didn't have the slightest interest in the family business—none of it.

And no one in the family understood that.

All his life, he'd had the Carey legacy hanging out in front of him like a hoop he was expected to jump through. Some people, he supposed, would have looked at that as a promise of a future. A path stretched out in front of him, all tidily laid out.

For Justin, though, that path led nowhere he wanted to be. He loved his family, but the thought of spending every day of his life behind a desk felt like a jail sentence. And he'd learned early that trying to please the family was, for him, a lesson in futility. As the youngest Carey sibling, he found that everyone had an opinion on what he should be doing. Despite loving his family, the only way he wouldn't eventually resent them for trying to rule his life was to strike out on his own.

To find his own way to contribute to the Carey Corporation.

And now he had it. He was almost ready to show his family that he was more than simply "the youngest."

"Okay, let's talk about the summer concert series," Bennett said, and slowly, the conversation began to quiet down.

Sunlight filled the room, but thanks to the wall of tinted windows, the light was muted. On the walls were framed family photos, plus pictures of the Carey Center, the restaurant and the shopping center. One day, Justin told himself, there would be framed pictures of *his* contribution to the family business. He was looking forward to that.

"Everything's on track, Bennett," Amanda said, still flipping through the bridal magazine.

"Thanks for your attention, Mandy," Bennett said wryly.

She lifted her gaze to his. "This is not the first time I've run our summer concert series, Bennett. I've got every evening filled. Our returning acts are happy to be here and the new ones are eagerly anticipating performing at the famed Carey Center.

"Ticket sales are through the roof, and I have to say…we've got the blueprints done for the pub and mall walk between the center and the new restaurant we're planning, and they're fantastic."

"When does work start on the new project?" Bennett watched her.

"Hannah did the first go-through, as you know…"

Bennett nodded.

"And since she's busy building Alli's castle and the retaining wall at Jack's place, we found another contractor to handle the beginnings of the job. We should break ground next month."

"Good news," Bennett said. "Hannah's going to be finished with the castle in a couple of weeks, but she's got jobs lined up now for the next two months. Not to mention that she's got some of her guys at my house, adding a breakfast room to the kitchen and painting every wall in the place."

"Hurray," Amanda said. "No more beige."

"Funny," Bennet countered.

"Anyway." Amanda nodded at their sister. "Serena's got a few new points about the Summer Stars program, but as for me, things are rolling." She took a breath, narrowed her eyes on him and reminded him, "I'm also getting married in a few months and I need time to plan the wedding."

"Right," he said, and shifted his gaze to his other sister. "Okay, then. Serena. The Summer Stars winners. Have we got them set up to perform this summer?"

She nodded her head at him and her butterscotch-blond hair flew around her shoulders. "Of course we do, Bennett. Do you think I'm incompetent?"

"What? No. Of course not." Bennett looked around the table and Justin couldn't help but think he looked like a man searching for a way out. "I'm just trying to be—"

"Controlling?" Serena asked, slowly pushing to her feet. "What is it about men that makes them think they have all the answers and the rest of us are just their cheering sections?"

"I don't think—"

"You're all alike," Serena said and Justin winced when he saw his softhearted sister's eyes fill with tears.

"Hey," Bennett said, standing up himself. "I'm not trying to control you, Serena. But I can if you want me to."

"Honestly, Bennett, you could *try* to be supportive." Amanda jabbed her index finger at her brother. "You all stick together. No matter what."

"What's going on?" Martin asked.

"No idea," Candace said and looked worriedly at her daughter.

"Bennett…" Justin looked at his sisters and then said, "maybe we should all calm down for a second and—"

"You stay out of this," Serena said and swiped a stray tear off her cheek. "You're never here, Justin, and now you just take Bennett's side against me?"

"I'm not taking sides," he protested, glancing at his brother as if looking for help. But Bennett was just as confused.

"Whose side am I supposed to be on?" Bennett demanded, confusion stamped on his features. "What are you talking about?"

"Jack," she said shortly. "Of course it's Jack. He wants to get married this summer and there's no time. It's *already* summer, for heaven's sake. I want to wait until Christmas…"

"Sure, because you don't have anything to do around Christmas," Justin muttered.

"You're on Jack's side, too," Serena said.

"Sweetie," Candace said softly. "This isn't a tragedy. We'll come up with something."

"I just can't deal with any of this today." Serena walked out of the room and Amanda watched her leave.

"See what you did? I can't believe you're this insensitive, Bennett. Has Hannah seen this side of you?" Amanda picked up her bridal magazine. "It's very unattractive."

She flounced out after Serena and Bennett looked at Justin. "What the hell just happened? How the hell did I go from asking about the Summer Stars to being insensitive?"

"Damned if I know." Justin looked at Candace. "Mom, do you have a clue what's going on?"

Slowly, Candace pushed to her feet, looked at

both of her sons, then shifted a brief glance at her husband. "What's going on is that once again, you men refuse to hear us. And sadly, that includes Jack and most probably Henry, as well. I suppose none of you can help it. It's simply your gender."

"Wait a minute," Martin said, standing. "How did I get lumped into this?"

"You're a man and you don't listen. How are you not in this?" Candace turned and left the room behind her daughters and Martin was just a step or two behind her.

Justin looked at Bennett. "What the hell did *we* do?"

"We were born male. Happy you were here to share the heat this time."

"Right," Justin said. "*Really* glad I made the time to come to this family meeting."

Scowling, Bennett said, "Maybe if you came more often, you'd be able to help me deal with our sisters."

"Yeah, no thanks." Justin grinned, shoved his hands into his jacket pockets and said, "You're the CEO. It's your job to handle the crap."

"I didn't see that in the contract," Bennett mumbled.

"Dad made you sign a contract?"

"Never mind." Bennett shook his head, eased one hip against the table and asked, "Why did you come to the meeting today, anyway? Which just so happened to turn into the shortest family meeting in history, thank-you to all the tiny business gods."

Justin laughed shortly. This was a side of his older brother he hadn't known existed. "Damn, Bennett, I've never known you to *not* like those meetings. What's happened to you?"

One corner of Bennett's mouth lifted and his gaze softened. "I found Hannah and discovered what having an actual *life* is like."

Hannah Yates, contractor and, apparently, *brother tamer.* He'd only met her the once at a big, splashy dinner at The Carey—the family corporation's flagship restaurant that Hannah and her crew had completely restored after a fire. But even meeting her only that night, Justin had seen the change she'd brought about in his brother.

And hell, if Bennett Carey could change, anything was possible.

Smiling to himself, Justin said, "I only came to thank you in person for loaning me that money a few weeks ago. I had the accountant cut you a check today to pay you back." He handed it over and was silently grateful to the grandfather who had left each of the Carey siblings a substantial trust. Still, there were hoops to jump through when you needed to draw on that money. He hadn't had time to wait and Bennett had come through for him when he'd needed it most. Justin wouldn't forget it.

Bennett dropped the check onto the table, crossed

his arms over his chest and said, "Uh-huh. Do I get to know why you needed it?"

Justin grinned. He'd been working this deal for three months. Hell, longer, if you considered he first tried to pull it off a year and a half ago.

But it didn't matter how long it had taken, he told himself. The point was, it was a done deal now. He'd turned over the cash payment just a couple of weeks ago and there was no going back. His course was set; now he just had to prove to everyone that he knew what he was doing. That starting a new branch of the Carey Corporation was the right thing for him.

"Earth to Justin."

"What?" He'd drifted off.

"I asked," Bennett said, "do I now get to know why you needed the money? Why you've been so damn secretive the last few months about what you're doing?"

He still wasn't ready to tell the family.

Bennett sighed. "It's a no. I can see it on your face."

"Yeah, it's a no. Today," Justin hedged. "But soon, Bennett."

"Yeah." Bennett laughed. "I've heard that a lot from you. Yet nothing changes."

Justin bristled a little. "It will, though, Bennett. You'll see soon enough."

This was the problem with being the youngest in the family. Everyone felt like they had a say in his life. They wanted to "help," but too often it ended up simply that they tried to steer him onto what they considered a safe path.

Well, Justin wasn't interested in "safe." He didn't care about doing the expected thing. What he did want was to carve out his own path. To prove to his family, at last, that in spite of not toeing the company line, he was a Carey.

Right down to the bone.

A couple of hours later, Justin was exactly where he wanted to be.

He stood on a slate patio and stared out at the wide sweep of the Pacific stretched out in front of him. Heavy, gray clouds hovered on the horizon and were busily sailing closer. And behind him was the hotel that would be his link in the Carey family chain.

Everything was riding on this. He'd taken a stand years ago—not against his family, but against being dragged into the family business. And this was his chance to prove to everyone that he'd been right to do it.

Here in La Jolla, just a few miles from San Diego, he was a good two hours from Orange County, California, where the Carey family had centered their world. Here, he wasn't the youngest Carey sibling. Here he was whoever the hell he wanted to be.

He was never going to be satisfied with sitting

behind a desk and moving from meeting to meeting. That kind of life felt more like a cage to Justin than anything else. It suited his family completely and they shone at running the corporation and growing it, as well.

He loved his family but he'd always felt like the proverbial square peg trying to find his way into a round hole. Eventually, he'd stopped trying and made the decision to go his own way.

His family didn't understand; they still saw him as the black sheep. The rebel. But once he told them what he was doing, maybe that would change. Maybe.

While the cold ocean breeze blew past him, ruffling his hair, tugging at the black leather jacket he wore, Justin heard the echoes of the last of that morning's conversation with his older brother.

"You've been avoiding the family for months, Justin. It's time to tell us all what you're up to."

"I will. Soon."

"That's what you said last month."

As the youngest of the four Carey siblings, Justin was used to the family trying to either rein him in or give him "advice" about how to run his own damn life. This time, he wasn't going to tell them anything about his plans until they were already set in stone.

He loved his family. All of them. But this he had to do for himself.

"I'm almost ready, Bennett," he said. "Believe me, I want you all to know."

"Fine." Bennett's sigh was both patient and irritated. Justin didn't know how he managed that. "I'm glad you came today. You might try coming to more family meetings."

Now it was Justin's turn to sigh. "I'm not part of the Carey Corporation, Bennett."

"You're part of the Carey family, Justin. Time you started acting like it."

Remembering the exchange, Justin rolled his shoulders as if shrugging off Bennett's last barb. It had stung, because there had been plenty of truth to it. He did miss the family. And he wasn't trying to cut himself off from them. But until he was firmly entrenched in his own business, he would steer clear. As he had been.

Justin stared out at the churning sea and watched waves crash against the shore, then ripple along the sand, leaving damp, lacy patterns in their wake. Sandpipers scuttled along the wet sand, leaving tiny footprints behind until the water washed them away.

Why the hell would he want to be at a meeting in Carey corporate headquarters when he could be standing here, between the sea and the hotel that would be his contribution to the Carey legacy?

No fabulous Carey Center for him. He admired what his family had built—basically a temple to the arts—but it wasn't *his*. It had never pulled at him the way it had his siblings. Hell, even his sister Serena had eventually become a part of the company, and from what he was told, she was damn good at it. But Justin wanted—needed—to make his own mark. And in that way, he realized, he was just like his father and older brother. They might not see it, but he did.

They'd made their mark *on* the Carey Center. He'd make his on the outside. Each of them did things their own way.

And here was where he was going to do it.

"Hey," a voice called out from behind him. "I've been looking for you for a half hour."

Thoughts shattered, Justin turned around and smiled as Sam Jonas walked up to join him. Tall and lanky, with long blond hair, wearing worn jeans and a faded red T-shirt, Sam looked just what he was: a surfer. Of course, he was also half owner of Jonas and Son Builders and was currently running the restoration of the hotel.

"Hey, Sam."

"Should have known I'd find you out here," Sam said and lifted his face into the sea wind, letting his hair stream out like a white blond flag behind him.

"Hard to resist," Justin admitted. On the ocean, there were a few surfers, and a couple of small sailboats skimming the surface, gem-colored sails ballooned out with the wind. And those storm clouds hustled even closer. "A hell of a view."

"It is that."

Five years ago, he'd met Sam outside a pub in Ireland, when they were both on solitary backpacking trips across Europe. As the only two Americans around, they'd bonded pretty quickly and spent the next couple of months traveling together.

Their friendship endured long after the trip had ended. Sam had gone into business with his father and now Jonas and Son Builders operated out of San Diego. While Justin had no interest in his family's business, he found himself sometimes envying Sam for being able to do what he loved and still please his family.

"Why were you looking for me?"

"What? Oh." Nodding, Sam said, "I wanted to let you know the designers are at work in the finished hotel rooms."

"Good news." With the front half of the hotel— the ocean-view side—nearly ready to open, and the rest of the rooms being upgraded quickly, the whole place would be ready for the public by the end of the month.

Damn good thing, since it felt as if he'd been building toward this moment for more than a year.

"Here's more," Sam told him. "The treatment rooms are finished, too, but for the light fixtures, and those are going in this afternoon."

"Seriously? Damn, man, you don't waste time,"

Justin said, smiling. He leaned his forearms on the iron railing and stared into the cold wind.

"You don't pay me to waste time, buddy," Sam pointed out. "We'll need another week or two to get the saunas and the pool where we want it, but everything else is up and about ready to shine."

"I'm going to owe you a bottle of scotch, aren't I?"

"Damn straight." Sam gave him a light punch on the shoulder. "Single malt, at least fifteen years old and preferably from the Highlands."

Justin laughed. "Got it. Anything else?"

"Actually, yeah," Sam said thoughtfully. "Once you're open, I want one of your best rooms for a long weekend."

Still laughing, Justin looked at him. "Seriously? You want one of the rooms?"

"Not for me. For Kate."

Kate O'Hara, OB nurse and Sam's fiancée. "For her? You got it, man. Best room in the house." Grinning, Justin added, "I still don't understand how she could have picked you over me."

"A woman of excellent taste," Sam quipped, then rubbed one hand against the center of his chest. "Can't believe the wedding's in three weeks."

"You're not nervous, are you?" Justin grinned.

"Hell no." Sam shrugged. "Nervous doesn't cover it. Scared half to death. What's wrong with eloping? Why do I have to stand in front of a couple hundred people?"

"Because that's what Kate wants and you're crazy about her."

A second or two later, Sam nodded. "I really am." He shot Justin a look. "So, as best man, you have the bachelor party all worked out?"

"Oh, yeah. It's going to be epic." As soon as he set it up. Damn it, he'd been so busy he'd forgotten all about that. But that was easily enough taken care of.

"And it's not the night before the wedding, right? Kate's being picky," he added. "Doesn't want me getting married with a hangover."

"Women." Justin slapped his friend on the back. "Don't worry about it. I'll have you at the wedding stone-cold sober."

"Yeah, that might not be a good idea, either."

Laughing, Justin half turned at a sound, a scent, some sense of motion. He swore every nerve ending in his body stood straight up the moment he spotted her. The bottom dropped out of his stomach and a slow burn started a bit lower.

Sam shifted to look at whatever Justin was staring at, then said, "Okay, then. Guess I'll get back to work."

"What? Oh." Hell, one look at her and Justin had forgotten his friend was standing right beside him. "Okay. Talk to you later."

Sam left and on his way past the woman headed Justin's way, he said, "Morning, Sadie."

She smiled but once he'd gone past, that smile slipped away and she faced Justin with the same cool expression he was getting used to.

Sadie Harris.

The one woman he'd never been able to get out of his mind. The one woman who still made guest spots in his dreams. The one woman who looked at him with a dismissive stare that Justin was just contrary enough to enjoy.

Sadie.

"Hello, Justin."

That soft, husky voice rippled through him and set off a ripple of heat he was pretty sure would immolate him any second.

It would be a hell of a way to go.

Two

"Hello, Justin."

Her voice was low, and made him remember all the nights they'd spent together. Just a year and a half ago, they'd been together during long nights when she would whisper his name while she wrapped those long legs around him.

"Sadie," he said.

She took a spot at the railing, keeping about two feet of space between them. Justin had to ask himself why her indifferent attitude was so damned attractive. Tall, she stood almost five foot ten and, he swore, most of that was legs. Long, shapely and tanned, it had been her legs he'd noticed first and he knew that every straight male would say the same.

But it was her eyes that held him. Big, brown with tiny flecks of gold in their centers, they were wary, watchful, suspicious even, and damned if he wasn't intrigued every time they met his. Her hair was thick, the color of good whiskey—brown with sun-kissed, amber streaks, and right now, that heavy mass of waves tumbled free to the middle of her back. He knew what it felt like in his hands and he wanted to feel it again.

She'd changed since he'd first met her. Her breasts were fuller, hips rounder, as if she'd gained a little weight in all the right places. He'd been back here the last few months and from the first time he'd seen her again, she'd been tormenting him. Whether she meant to or not. Just looking at her kindled a fire in the pit of his belly. This woman had always turned him inside out and made him hunger for the heat they'd once found together.

But now Sadie was a hell of a lot pricklier than the first time they'd met. She wore pale, cream-colored shorts, a tight, mint green T-shirt and sandals. And she made that simple outfit look staggering. He waited until she turned to look him in the eye and when their gazes locked, he felt the snap of heat like a gut punch.

She closed her hands over the damp, icy railing and shifted her gaze to the sea. Almost, he thought, as if she couldn't bear looking at him. She hadn't always been that way, though. When they'd met more than a year ago, they hadn't been able to keep their hands off each other.

Back then, there was nothing cool in her eyes when she looked at him. It had been heat. The kind of soul-swamping heat that made a man believe in heaven.

But apparently, things had changed.

"We've been working together now for a couple of months," Justin said. "You want to tell me why you still treat me like the enemy? All of this—this whole project—is because of you. And your father," he added. "You're the one who came to me, remember?"

She tipped her face into the ocean wind and he watched that breeze lift her hair into a dark cloud, swirling around her. Tempting, that was what she was. Just pure temptation brought to life.

"I remember," she said finally. "That doesn't mean I'm happy about it."

A man with two sisters knew how complicated and yet, Justin had to admit that what was between him and Sadie was even more so. He hadn't seen her for a year and a half when she'd called him three months ago with an offer he couldn't refuse. Sounded like a movie plot, but it was the truth. But from that unexpected phone call to this minute, she'd been so coldly polite Justin spent most of his days with frostbite.

And he had no idea why she was so clearly furious. He'd left it alone until now, figuring that at some point, she'd tell him why she was so angry. But she hadn't and he was tired of living with an ax hanging over his head.

The worst of it was, he still wanted her.

"Is the attitude because you needed help?" he finally asked, honestly curious. "Or because you needed help from *me*?"

"Good question," she murmured and then slanted a look at him. "I think it's you."

"Great. Progress." He leaned his forearms on the railing and kept his distance as he asked, "And why's that? You're still pissed because I left?"

"Please." She laughed a little, but didn't sound amused. "Don't think so highly of yourself."

One eyebrow lifted. It wasn't much of a conversation, but at least she was talking to him. "Okay, fine. Then why?"

"Really, Justin? You can't figure out what I'm experiencing here?" Sadie's eyes flashed and that was the most emotion he'd seen from her since he'd come back to San Diego. Hell, even if she was mad, at least he knew she was feeling *something*.

She slapped one hand on the iron railing and turned to face him. "Let's think," she said tightly. "Maybe it's because I didn't want to sell our family hotel but had no choice?" She whipped her hair back behind her shoulders and glared at him. "Could that have something to do with it?"

"Like I said, Sadie. Nobody forced you to call me, right? Coming back here wasn't my idea, remember?"

"Oh, trust me, Justin," she countered. "I remember that you never came back."

"Here we go," he muttered.

"No." She interrupted him with a quick shake of her head. "It's you coming in and making all these changes…"

"You wanted to renovate."

"Of course, but I want to keep some of the history, too. This is my family's place. My great-grandfather's legacy and too much of it is changing."

He sighed, scrubbed one hand across his face and quickly tried to find a way to say what needed saying. Without also pushing Sadie even further away than she was already.

A year and a half ago, Justin had tried to buy the beautiful old hotel and after a couple of weeks of talks and negotiations that went nowhere, she and her father had turned him down flat. Justin had been searching since for the kind of place that could compete with the Cliffside, but he'd never found another one like it.

Then out of nowhere, three months ago, Sadie had called him to open negotiations again. He hadn't understood what had changed her mind, and truthfully, at the time, all he was thinking about was getting his hands on the Cliffside so he hadn't cared. Now, though, he wanted a few answers.

"We are keeping some of the history. But faded wallpaper has got to go. Besides, again," Justin reminded her, "you called me with the offer."

"Because I had no choice." She sighed, and briefly turned her gaze to the ocean before facing him again.

Justin understood that. Her father had been sick and she'd needed money fast to get him settled and pay off some of the bills that were coming in. Had Justin taken advantage of the situation? No, he didn't think so. She had needed him, and the deal they'd finally hammered out was more than fair.

Still, he knew what the hotel meant to her—and her family. As she'd said, it was the Harris legacy. The old place had been in her family for decades, and as a Carey, he knew what that kind of tradition could mean. It wasn't only a responsibility but a burden of sorts, weighing her down and making her consider and reconsider every decision she made.

"I get that. Had to be hard to swallow, but we all do what we have to do." He watched her. "With that in mind, how's your dad feeling?"

She sighed and he didn't know if it was exasperation or resignation. "He's much better. Thanks."

He liked her dad a lot and he was worried the

man had been hit with a medical issue. But Justin wasn't sorry he'd gotten the hotel. And he couldn't regret being back here. With Sadie.

"We're a team now, Sadie," he finally said. "Whether you like it or not."

"A team." Her lips twisted into a sardonic smile that tore at him.

He took a step toward her and stopped when she looked at him as if she were going to turn and bolt. "You realize that you'll have to get used to having me around. Dealing with me."

"Oh, believe me," she muttered, turning her face toward the sea rather than look at him. "I know."

A year or so ago, she'd been in his bed and hadn't seemed to have a problem with him being around at all. Hell, just remembering the nights with Sadie could make him hard and hot, in spite of that icy sea wind whirling around him. Staring at her profile now, Justin was forced to admit that it didn't seem her memories were as pleasant as his.

Or she was lying to herself.

Scowling at the thoughts tumbling through his mind, Justin half turned to look over his shoulder at the reason he was willing to put up with Sadie's bad attitude and the memories that wouldn't leave him alone.

The Cliffside Hotel. It was practically an institution in La Jolla, California. Just eleven miles from San Diego, La Jolla boasted some of the best coastline in the state. The world-famous Torrey Pines Golf Course was close by and sat on the edge of cliffs overlooking the pounding ocean. Just beyond the hotel, the village of La Jolla was filled with art galleries, five-star restaurants and exclusive boutiques. That tiny town drew tourists from all over the world, and soon, the Cliffside Hotel and Spa would be able to compete with the best resorts the village had to offer.

Along the shore there were tide pools to explore and La Jolla Cove, a small, deep-water bay that drew experienced and novice snorkelers from all over to explore the sea caves.

The Cliffside itself sat right on the beach. Landscaping that needed some care lined the front of the sprawling building, and the restaurant was a wall of glass that faced the sea. Three stories of rooms spread out from that restaurant and formed a horseshoe so that each room had a balcony with either a view of the ocean, or one of the village and the spacious gardens that filled the hotel courtyard and lay behind it in a riot of color year round.

The Cliffside had stood on this spot for more than sixty years, and while it was still spectacular, it was beginning to look a little haggard. Sea air and salt spray had done a number on the paint, and the wide porch needed to be redone in cedar so it would stand up to the dampness.

All it needed was some freshening and redesigning of the rooms to make them more contemporary while still holding on to the history the hotel had earned. Which was why Justin had first come to the hotel more than a year ago. And why Sadie had called him back.

"Damn it, Sadie, we both know this is a good deal for both of us." He took a step closer and stopped when she shifted to face him. "We can work together or you can keep up the ice woman treatment."

She laughed a little, but the humor didn't reach her eyes and that was a little disappointing. Because he remembered what a great laugh she had, and how her eyes would shine with it.

"Ice woman," she repeated. "I sort of like that."

"Of course you do." Reaching out, he almost touched her hand, but she slid it back on the black railing and Justin sighed.

"Fine," he said. "But if that's the way you want to play this it's going to make for a hard partnership."

"Partners?"

"We both own the hotel, so yeah. Partners."

Shaking her head, she looked at him for a long moment before saying, "You with seventy-five percent and me with twenty-five isn't exactly an equal partnership."

"I didn't say it was equal," he pointed out and gave her a smile that got zero reaction from her. "Look, paperwork's been signed. You got your cash payout a couple weeks ago, so why the attitude today?"

Sadie slapped one hand on the railing lining the slate patio. When she looked at him, she said, "Because I didn't want to make the deal."

"Yeah," Justin said with a half smile. "You made that pretty clear when I was here a year and a half ago."

"Fifteen months," she corrected.

Three months made that big a difference? One eyebrow winged up. "That's very specific. Do you have it down to days and hours, too?"

"You might be surprised."

Her face was unreadable, and still he stared at her. Those eyes drew him as they had from the first moment they met. And even at times like now, when she was coldly angry, he couldn't deny the craving she caused. And he had to wonder, if he reached for her now, pulled her in tight and kissed her, would she push him away? Or kiss him back?

He wasn't sure he wanted to know. For the moment.

Changing the subject, he said, "The designers are finishing up with the ocean-view rooms."

"Yes, I know. I walked through a few of them before I came down here."

Wryly, he said, "Tamp down the excitement, Sadie. It's embarrassing." He laughed shortly. "We used most of your ideas on those rooms. I would have thought you'd sound more pleased with the results."

"Of course I'm pleased about them," she said. "I've wanted to fix up the rooms for a long time. Dad and I talked about this for years, too, you know. It wasn't all your brilliant idea to come swooping in with plans. We just couldn't do it earlier." She looked into his eyes and said simply, "As for using my designs? They were good and you know it, so don't act as if you were doing me a favor."

"I wasn't…"

She cut him off. "Fifteen months ago, you came here and made an offer for our hotel."

"And you said no," he added, before she could. "Things change."

Swiping one hand through her hair, she held it back from her face. "Yes. This time we sold it. But it wasn't by choice. There was no other option."

"Maybe not. But you were happy enough about the cash payout," he reminded her. "You liked the indoor pool and the swim spa you talked me into."

She waved at him. "That was brilliant and you know it. Clients will love it."

He'd already acknowledged that she was right about the swim spa.

"My point," he ground out, "is that you've had plenty of say in what we're doing. Hell, you sold the place to me and still managed to hang on to twenty-five percent of it," he said. "*That* should make you happy if nothing else does."

He hadn't liked her terms, Hadn't thought to have a partner. But they'd been set in stone as far as she was concerned, so he'd accepted it because this hotel was going to be the start of something for him. Once the Cliffside established itself, he'd start over on another hotel that had been left to age less than gracefully.

Justin was going to prove that he'd done the right thing in walking away from the Carey Corporation and paving his own way. If that meant having to bargain on this, the first hotel of what would be many, then so be it.

"Oh, yes," Sadie said wryly. "Twenty-five percent of a hotel that was one hundred percent my family's up until a month ago." She shook her head. "Wait. Let me get the balloons."

Justin stared at her for a long minute. Putting aside the fact that she could set him on fire with a glance, she was a damn mystery. He'd liked that about her when they first met because he hadn't been looking long-term anyway. If she wanted to keep her secrets, then fine. Worked out better for both of them. Nothing wrong with a lot of lust and heat. Neither of them had been after hearts and flowers, after all.

But now they'd be working together. Joined by a contract that would make it impossible to *not* deal with each other. So the time for all the mystery was over.

He tucked his hands into his jacket pockets, braced his legs wide apart and tipped his head to one side to study her. "We used to like each other, Sadie."

"Like?" she repeated. "That's what you think? We liked each other?"

"Didn't we?" Now he was confused and maybe more than a little irritated. "I liked you and the way I remember it, you seemed pretty fond of me, too."

"More than fond and you know it." She inhaled sharply. "At least until you disappeared."

He remembered. But he'd done what he'd had to do. "I *left*. There's a difference."

"Sure," she said, sounding way too amiable for the glint in her eyes. "You *left* my bed to take a shower, you said, and then you *left* without another word."

He scrubbed one hand across his face. She was right, but he hadn't seen it that way at the time. He'd had to go because if he'd stayed any longer he might never have left. She'd been too important to him and he hadn't been able to embrace that because he'd had to make his way. Find his path before he indulge himself in a relationship. "Damn it, Sadie. I didn't want to hurt you. But I couldn't stay."

"Well, that's okay, then. Thanks so much."

"We had an affair, Sadie. Hot. Sexy as hell and

temporary," he said tightly, defending himself against the accusation he saw in her eyes. "Neither of us made promises."

That was certainly true, Sadie told herself. No promises, just the magic of being with him. The thrill of his touch and the hunger he aroused in her like no other man ever had—or would. And then it had all gone to hell.

"No. We didn't." Sadie Harris sighed and realized that talking about this wasn't doing any good. It surely wasn't making her feel any better. But she'd been holding on to these feelings for a long time. Was it so bad to dump some of them on him now that she had the chance?

Just looking at him made her blood burn and her heart beat faster. Harder. She remembered every minute of every night she'd spent with him what felt like a lifetime ago. The sensation of his hands sliding over her body. The heat of his breath as he suckled at her breasts and the amazing friction when his body slid into hers. She trembled and Sadie locked her knees so she wouldn't simply sink to the pavement.

Justin's light brown, sun-streaked hair was a little too long, curling over his collar, making her want to touch, to wind her fingers through it. His pale blue eyes shone like ice chips, yet she knew exactly what they looked like when they were reflecting the heat burning between them. His jaw carried a couple days' worth of scruff, only adding to the ridiculously attractive package.

He wore that black leather jacket—Armani, of course—that he loved so much, over a black T-shirt and black jeans. His black boots were scuffed and scarred and somehow just right. He was tall, well over six feet, ensuring that she had to look up at him in spite of her five feet ten inches of height. She suspected he enjoyed that.

God, she'd missed him.

And that was a dangerous thought to entertain, however briefly.

Fifteen months ago, she'd spent two weeks with Justin Carey and they'd been the best two weeks of her life. He was funny and smart and there was an innate kindness in him that had attracted her from the start. Of course, the fact that he could set her hair on fire with a kiss didn't hurt anything, either.

But when he left that last morning and didn't even bother to *wave* at her, she'd been crushed. No, they hadn't made promises to each other, but they'd been so good together that she'd allowed herself to hope—to believe—that there was more between them than simple heat.

She was wrong.

"Here's the deal," he was saying and she looked into the blue eyes she'd never forgotten. "We don't have to be friends, Sadie. But damned if I'm going to have a partner I'm at war with every day. So why don't you just tell me what's bugging you and get it over with?"

God, she thought. Where to begin? With the lie? Or the truth?

She took a deep breath and steeled herself for what was to come. "You need me to satisfy your curiosity?"

He shrugged. "Why not?"

"Because I don't owe you anything, Justin." At least, she'd been telling herself that for the last fifteen months. She hoped it was true. Hoped she'd done the right thing.

"Didn't say you did, but you might want to reconsider since we *are* partners now."

She shook her head and when her hair flew across her eyes, she impatiently plucked it free. "Only as far as the hotel goes."

"Well, yeah. What other way is there?"

Sadie laughed lightly. "Fifteen months and you haven't changed a bit."

"What's that supposed to mean? Sort of sounds like I should be insulted."

"The hotel was all you could see then and it's the same now."

"That's why I'm here," he pointed out. "The hotel is why you called me. What the hell else am I supposed to be seeing?"

"Never mind, Justin," she said and half turned to

leave until he laid one hand on her arm to hold her there. The heat of his touch sank into her bones and drifted crazily throughout her body.

"Just wait."

She lifted her gaze to his and stared into those pale blue eyes, wishing things were different. Wishing they could start over somehow. Wishing...never did anyone any good.

"What the hell is wrong here, Sadie? The way I remember it, we got along great a year and a half ago."

"Fifteen months," she muttered.

"Fine," he said flatly. "Fifteen months. My point was, we had a good time together."

"And then you left," she countered.

"Well, yeah." Justin let her go, then pushed one hand through his hair. "I wanted your family's hotel. You wouldn't sell. Why would I stay?"

Sadie tipped her head to one side and studied him. She wouldn't have thought it possible, but he looked even better than he had fifteen months ago.

"Right," she said finally. "You had no reason to stay. We were just together every night for two weeks."

"Is that what this is about?" He shook his head and gave a half laugh. "Damn, Sadie. We both knew what we were doing. It was an affair. A damned hot one," he added with a wink that she guessed was supposed to be charming, "but an affair. Nobody said anything about me staying forever."

"Who asked for forever?" Sadie demanded. She'd known going into those two weeks with Justin Carey that it wouldn't last. How could it? He wasn't in La Jolla looking to build a life. He'd only been there trying to *buy* her life. Yet, even knowing that, she'd dreamed a lot of what-ifs. "How about a simple *Bye, Sadie. It's been fun*." She pushed her windblown hair back from her face with impatient hands. "You couldn't even manage that. One morning, you were just…gone."

"Is *that* what's been bugging you for weeks now?" He shoved his hands into his jacket pockets. "I had to go. Family crap I had to deal with."

"And you couldn't tell me that?"

He sighed. "Yeah. I could have. Maybe should have, I don't know." His gaze speared into hers. "But there was no reason for me to stay, Sadie. You know that. You and your dad refused to sell the hotel and my reason for being here evaporated."

"We had something, Justin," she said. "Even if all it deserved was a goodbye, we had *something*."

"We had a good time," he said and lifted one hand to touch her, but Sadie stepped back.

Fifteen months without him and now he was back. She'd sold him the hotel, so he wouldn't be going anywhere. With her father so sick, she'd needed the money Justin paid her. And maybe she could have gotten more from someone—anyone else. But she hadn't had time to shop around for a buyer. Instead, she'd called the man she already knew wanted the hotel. It was time for Justin to understand just what had happened while he was gone.

"We did," she said. "And now you're back."

"Not going anywhere."

"Right. So." She took a breath, shifted her gaze briefly to the ocean before turning back to him again. The man she'd never forgotten. The man who visited her dreams and left her every morning aching and wanting. The man who had changed her life.

"So?"

"We should talk, Justin."

"Thought we were," he quipped.

She ignored that. "You haven't asked me how I am. If anything's new."

He frowned, clearly confused. "Okay. How are you, Sadie? What's new?"

Here it was. Time to rip off the Band-Aid. She blew out a breath and said, "I'm fine, thanks for asking. As for what's new? Well, he's six months old now, so not really new. But newish."

Justin went still. When he spoke again, his voice was tight and low. "*Who* is six months old?"

"Your son," she said, watching those pale blue eyes. "*Our* son."

Three

He held up one hand. "I'm sorry. *What?*"

"Our son. Ethan." Just saying her baby's name brought a smile to Sadie's face, but it dissolved quickly enough in the flash of heat in Justin's eyes.

"*Our* son. Ethan," he said.

She took a breath. "This is going to take forever if you just keep repeating what I'm telling you."

"Six months old?" he demanded.

"Yes."

He scrubbed both hands across his face. "You had a baby. *My* baby."

Since she could see Justin in her son's face, there

would be no denying it even if she wanted to. And yet. "Yes. Well, *my* baby."

He shoved both hands through his hair, then just held his head as if afraid it would explode. "What the hell, Sadie? You didn't bother to tell me that I'm a damn father?"

"No, I didn't. And you didn't bother to say good-bye when you left."

He choked out a laugh. "Seriously? You're comparing those two things and saying it's what? Fair?"

She'd struggled with whether to tell him or not. Those long months of pregnancy had been some of the loneliest of her life. Oh, she'd had her parents who were supportive, though her father had wanted to confront Justin on his own and only Sadie's fast talking had stopped him. But she'd experienced the joys, the fears, the magic of those nine months as the single mother she would be. Maybe she should have told him. Maybe. But when they were together, he'd made it very clear that he wasn't looking for a long-term relationship.

And to be fair, she hadn't been looking, either. At first.

But after the first week with Justin, Sadie had begun to want more.

After he left, she'd discovered that was exactly what she'd gotten.

God, she hadn't meant to just blurt out the truth like this. The plan had been to ease him into knowing about Ethan. But the truth had been gnawing at her for the last two months. Not to mention the difficulty of keeping Ethan out of Justin's way. Being this close to Justin again, knowing what he'd missed, knowing what she'd kept from him, it had to come out.

In her defense, she thought, not telling him about the baby had made her feel terrible. But should she really have tracked him down to tell him she was pregnant, when he'd left so quickly and made it clear she wasn't important to him at all? And if she wasn't important, how could her son be?

No. She'd done the right thing.

Justin Carey's family had more money than she could even imagine. If he'd wanted to, he could have taken Ethan. He could have hired the best lawyers and she'd never have been able to afford a long court battle. She might have lost her son to a man who'd walked away from her without a second thought. And there was still a chance he would do just that— though she would fight him with everything she had.

So in the midst of her guilt, there was also a nugget of acceptance that she'd done the right thing.

"Where is he?"

Brought up out of her thoughts, her gaze snapped to his. "Safe."

"Seriously? Safe? That's all I get?" He threw both hands up. "You live here at the hotel. I've been in your suite. I didn't see him."

"I didn't want you to. Not until we'd talked."

"And 'talking' took you two months? We've been together nearly every day since this project started, Sadie. Yet, you never mentioned Ethan."

That hadn't been easy for her. So many times, she'd almost said it. Almost told him what they shared. With the hotel closed for renovations, Justin had paid their employees to take some time off, which was why no one had been able to spill her secret. Maybe knowing that she was safe from him finding out accidentally had given her the opportunity to keep quiet, to see if he was the man she remembered. "I had to find the right time."

"Sure. I'm not playing games with you, Sadie." Justin took a step toward her and stopped again. "If I have a son, I want to see him."

"If?" Of all the things she'd imagined him saying to her at this moment, that hadn't been one of them. "Why would I lie to you about that?"

"Good question," Justin snapped. "But you've been lying to me for... *fifteen months.*"

"I didn't lie," she muttered thickly. "I just didn't say anything."

"A fine distinction."

The fact that he was right made her cringe a little. "Justin, I don't want to fight with you about this."

"That's a damn shame." He stepped still closer and Sadie just managed to keep from stepping back.

But she wouldn't look weak even if she *felt* weak. She wanted to walk away from the entire situation.

She stared up into those eyes of his and thought she could actually see chips of ice floating in those pale blue depths.

"I want to see him."

"You will," Sadie said and lifted her chin slightly. "But not until you've calmed down."

He laughed, but there was no humor in the sound. "I just found out I have a son I knew nothing about and you want me to calm down?"

"Justin," she said, fighting for calm herself, "do you remember how you left last time you were here?"

"What's that have to do with anything?"

She gritted her teeth, took a deep breath and said, "Every night for two weeks, we were together."

He stared at her but didn't speak, so Sadie kept going.

She still couldn't believe how she'd reacted to him. Looking back now, it seemed that the moment they'd met, there had been some invisible force drawing them together. She'd never experienced anything like it before and hadn't since, either.

She wasn't a one-night-stand kind of woman, but with him, she hadn't been able to help herself. It was heat and passion and the best sex of her life, and she'd fallen, foolishly, in love. Thankfully, she'd gotten over that.

"I remember."

"And do you also remember that when my father finally said no to the sale, you disappeared?"

"I left. There's a difference."

"Not really," she argued, running with the chance to say what she'd been feeling for the last year and more. She'd loved him, allowed herself to dream of being with him always. She'd let herself believe that his touch, his whispers in the night meant that he loved her, too. She was wrong. "You left my room in the middle of the night and in the morning, you were just gone. Like you'd never been there at all." The sting of that could still bring a slow burn to the center of her chest. "No call. No note. No fond farewells. You just left without a backward glance."

He pushed one hand through his hair. "I never said I was going to stay, Sadie."

"No, you didn't. And I'm not even saying I wanted you to." Now she was lying, but he didn't need to know that.

"What are you saying, then?"

"That if you couldn't be bothered to even say goodbye to me, why would I think you would care about a surprise pregnancy?"

"Okay." He ran one hand over his face and nodded. "You might have a point there." He shook his head. "Two completely different things. And while we're at it, we used condoms. How the hell did you get pregnant?"

"They're not perfect."

"That's just great." He threw his hands up. "They've got one job and can't manage it." Still shaking his head, he walked away from her, stared out at the ocean for a long minute or two, then turned back to face her. "You had plenty of time, Sadie. You shouldn't have kept this from me. You had no right."

"I have every right," she argued. "He's my son and I'm not going to have him hurt by a father who might decide to just walk away one day."

He gave her a fierce scowl. "I wouldn't do that."

"Really?" She tipped her head to one side and looked at him. "You already did." She saw a quick flash of insult in his eyes and when he spoke, she heard regret in his voice.

"Damn it, Sadie. You should have told me."

Probably. She wrapped her arms around herself and held on as if giving herself a comforting hug. "I don't know, Justin. Maybe I should have. But if I could do it over, I don't know that I'd do it differently. Ethan's mine to protect."

"He's mine, too, Sadie. And I want to meet my son." He stared at her with speculation. "That's why you insisted on keeping twenty-five percent of the hotel. Because of the baby."

She sighed. "Mostly, yes. As long as your idea for transforming the hotel into a world-class spa resort works out, I'll never have to worry about taking care of Ethan."

He took the few steps separating them with a couple of long strides. She always had admired how he could look so fierce, so confident, sure of himself and what he wanted. Now those emotions were stamped on his features as he reached out and grabbed her upper arms.

"Did you really think I wouldn't take care of my son?"

"This isn't about what you would do, Justin. *I* take care of Ethan. *Me*." She pulled free. "This is just what I was worried about."

"What?"

"That you would sweep in here with your family name and money and try to take over. I don't need you to take care of Ethan," she said and jabbed her index finger at his chest. "We've been doing fine without you."

"Yeah, well. It doesn't matter what you want." His gaze narrowed on hers and she read fury and determination in those pale blue eyes. "I know the truth now and you're not keeping him away from me."

That sounded like a threat, and even if it wasn't, she knew it could have been. With the kind of money Justin's family had, she was at a serious disadvantage.

"So, where is he?"

The wind was icy, but it was not the source of the chill sliding up and down Sadie's spine. "In my suite."

"Let's go." He took her arm and turned her toward the hotel.

The burn of his touch filled her and yet still it wasn't enough to take away the chill of fear. Fear for her son. For her. For the life she'd built for them both. Sadie had known that asking Justin to come back to the hotel would be dangerous. That he would somehow tangle her up again, twisting her emotions into knots. But knowing that didn't make it any easier.

And even with those thoughts filling her mind, she looked at the hotel as they walked closer and noted all the changes Carey money had already made. New sun umbrellas in a bright red-and-white stripe over brand-new round tables and iron chairs with cream-colored cushions. The flagstone patio had been re-mortared and power-washed so that it sparkled in the sunlight.

New accordion doors opened from the patio into the main dining room so that it brought the outside in. The building itself was going to be painted in a few days and the terra cotta Spanish tiles on the roof had been replaced by the same kind of tile, but in an aquamarine color that mimicked the sea.

He'd made so many incremental changes that had ensured, on the whole, the hotel was sparkling. Her great-grandfather had built the place and for years, it had done good business, mostly because of its location. Not many hotels could boast of being right on the beach in La Jolla. But now people wanted more than just easy access to the ocean. They wanted an *experience* when it came to their hotel. They wanted to be pampered, and with the Cliffside's location, it was prime for just such a makeover.

Of course, her father had turned down Justin's offer fifteen months ago. He'd wanted, hoped, to make these changes himself. But then her dad got sick. He needed a heart operation and he needed to move somewhere warm and dry and relax for the first time in his life.

Which had left Sadie with few options, so she'd called Justin and reopened negotiations herself. His offer this time was substantially more—including the cash bonus she'd insisted on for her father's sake. Plus she'd kept an interest in her family's hotel, ensuring Ethan's future and hers. Not to mention being able to have a say in how her family's hotel was remade.

He had a tight grip on her upper arm and stalked along beside her while her brain kept spinning. Maybe because she was trying to not think about him and Ethan together. About having to trust Justin with her son's heart. Of having to trust Justin, period.

To give him his due, though, Justin hadn't wasted any time, once he owned the hotel. He'd been in San Diego off and on for the last three months, pouring money into the Cliffside and working with designers and with Sadie, to enhance their gym and to build "treatment rooms" for what would be the spa element.

When Justin Carey wanted something, nothing would stand in his way. He'd wanted her that way once and remembering his determination to get her into his bed was enough to shake her soul. Which was just another reason to be wary. If he decided he wanted his son—what was there to stop him?

Still holding on to her, Justin made his way to the elevators. Sadie finally pulled free, glanced at him and said, "I know the way. You don't have to perp-walk me."

"Fine. Let's go, then." He pushed the button, and when the elevator doors swished open, waved her inside.

She hit the button for the top floor, then stepped to the rear of the car, keeping a safe distance between them.

Justin watched her, and in spite of the circumstances, felt that familiar burn in his body. Sure, a lot of that heat at the moment was anger. But he couldn't deny the sexual pull he felt for her. It had been there from the moment he'd looked into those gold-flecked eyes and shook her hand fifteen months ago. There had been an electrical jolt of something undeniable the moment their hands met—and it was still there.

Being around Sadie had a way of putting pure

lust in charge of the thinking for him. He wanted her. Even now. Even knowing that she'd lied to him for almost a year and a half.

Studying her, he finally understood why her body looked riper, fuller than he'd remembered. She'd had a child. *His* child. That realization planted itself uppermost in his mind and even managed, briefly, to shove lust onto the back burner.

He was a father.

That thought was enough to send fear racing along his spine. Most men had nine long months to get used to the idea of having a tiny human depend on them. He'd had five minutes and it wasn't nearly long enough.

Assuming she was telling him the truth. But why would she lie now after keeping the whole thing a secret all this time? He'd have to do some checking on this. He'd want a DNA test—to be sure. But looking at her now, seeing the gleam of what looked like worry in her eyes, he was ready to believe her.

The doors opened and he waited for her to precede him into the hall. He knew her corner suite well. There were views of the ocean from both sides of the main room and both of the bedrooms. Those views were staggering enough that she used to never draw the drapes. Even at night, they were open to the flickering lights of La Jolla and the moon that dazzled the sea.

He didn't speak and neither did she on the walk

to her rooms. Hell, he didn't have a clue what to say. A father. The thought was terrifying and…intriguing, as well.

He'd always thought that someday, in the far distant, nebulous future, he would have children. A wife. A home. But it wasn't even on his radar now. He was still trying to forge his own path within his family. This was about doing what he needed to, to build his future. And he wondered if he'd be able to do this. Be a *father*? A *dad*? What if he screwed it all up? What if he was so bad at the parenting thing that his kid turned into a mean little bastard? Or worse? And that wasn't even considering the fact that now he would be tied forever to Sadie. That continuous, sexual pull he felt for her was going to be a permanent part of his life.

His sister Serena had always wanted to be a mother and now she had his niece, Alli, and was newly engaged to Jack Colton. Amanda Carey was engaged, as well, to Henry Porter, so he expected that at some point she would have a child, as well. And hell, even their older brother, Bennett, had fallen in love and was now engaged, and Hannah made no secret of the fact that she wanted a lot of kids.

Strange to realize that Justin was the one to provide the second grandchild to the Careys. Strange—and he wasn't ashamed to admit, a little terrifying.

Sadie used her key card, swung the door into the

well-appointed set of rooms and called out, "Mike. I'm back."

"Mike?" Justin stared at her. She had some guy in her suite? Some guy watching *his* son? She trusted some other guy to know Justin's son? To have a relationship with him? Was he also in a relationship with Sadie? Hell, he didn't like that at all. "Something else you want to tell me?"

Before Sadie could say anything, a young woman came out of one of the bedrooms holding a baby close. She had short blond hair, brown eyes and a suspicious gleam in her eyes as she looked at Justin. But he had eyes only for the tiny boy grinning and babbling incomprehensibly.

"Mike, this is Justin Carey." She paused. "Ethan's father. Justin, this is Michelle Franks. Mike works here at the hotel and helps me out with the baby."

He barely heard Sadie. The words sounded like those old Charlie Brown cartoons, where the parents' voices were just noise. That was what he heard while Sadie and Mike talked to each other. Justin couldn't tear his gaze from the baby. He walked closer and stared into a miniature face so like his own Justin couldn't think of a damn thing to say. Except the obvious, of course.

DNA test or not, this was his son.

There was simply no denying it. The boy even had Justin's pale blue eyes and one dimple in his left cheek. He was a mini-me, Justin told himself.

The question now was, what to do about it?

He didn't like not knowing. He much preferred having a plan.

"I don't even know what the hell to say," Justin admitted, and the minute the words came out of his mouth, he wanted to bite them back. He was rarely at a loss for words and on those few occasions, he hadn't admitted it. Especially to an adversary. And at the moment, that was exactly what Sadie Harris felt like.

"Justin, I know you're shocked," she said. "It's a lot to take in. But I don't want anything from you. Ethan and I are doing just fine. I only thought you should know."

"Because it was getting too hard to hide it with me right here?"

"Mostly," she admitted. "But not entirely."

He swiveled his head to give her a hard look. Hell, he'd thought he knew Sadie Harris. Those two weeks with her were what fantasies were made of. She was sexy and kind and funny and smart and, all in all, the perfect woman. Which was another reason he'd left so damn fast. He hadn't been ready for her. Hadn't been ready for that whispered *"I love you"* that had slipped from her their last night together.

Love? Forever? He'd had too much to prove. Too many things to do. So he'd left while he could.

"Fifteen months later," he said. "That's when you figured I should know." Justin fought to get a grip

on the anger churning inside him. Looking from her to the boy they shared, he tried to sort out the myriad emotions racing through him. How could he not have known he was a father? Shouldn't he have *sensed* it on some level? Hell, he'd helped create a new human and hadn't realized it.

His gaze locked on the baby and he felt his throat tighten. He and Sadie had made a child and he hadn't had a clue.

There had been times over the last year and a half when he'd thought about calling her. When he'd regretted leaving. When he'd wake up in the middle of the night aching for her. But he hadn't made that call because—hell, the reasons why didn't matter. Not now. Not when he was faced with a child who had his eyes. His smile. That dimple.

"Damn it, Sadie," he muttered, never taking his gaze from the tiny boy in front of him, "you had no right to keep this from me."

"Mike, you should go downstairs. See if they need any help."

"Are you sure?" the other woman asked as she handed the baby over to Sadie.

"We're fine. Thanks."

Justin waited until the woman was gone, then he speared Sadie with a glare and waited for some kind of damn explanation.

"Justin, you left." She met his gaze squarely and lifted her chin a little in defiance. "You never called.

You never came back. Why should I have thought that you'd be interested in my child if you clearly weren't interested in me?"

"Not just *your* child, Sadie."

"You made him, Justin, but you're not raising him."

"Whose fault is that?" he demanded. "I didn't know he existed. Until now."

He watched her eyes go wide, then narrow with suspicion even as she cuddled Ethan closer to her. "What's that mean?"

"I think you know what it means," he muttered and reached out to take the baby. Sadie hesitated, but finally released Ethan to him.

Justin held his breath as he settled his son on his arm. He half expected the tiny boy to let out a howl at having a stranger hold him. But he needn't have worried. Ethan stared at him for a long, breathless moment. Father and son studied each other and Sadie might as well have not been there. It was as if Justin were alone in the world with his son. Looking at *his son* was a staggering experience that he wouldn't have been able to describe to anyone.

The child was a solid weight that smelled of soap and baby powder. He wore a tiny red shirt with navy blue shorts over his diaper. His knees were dimpled and his bare feet kicked excitedly as if he was trying to run. Clapping his hands together, Ethan looked at his mother, then turned back to Justin and happily patted his daddy's cheeks.

And suddenly, something…happened.

Staring into his son's eyes—so much like his own—Justin felt his heart actually turn over in his chest. His pulse was pounding and his mouth and throat were so dry it felt as if he were choking. And maybe he was. The baby gave him a wide, toothless smile and slipped into Justin's soul with an ease that was breathtaking. How could a man steel himself against this kind of feeling? This wide, deep emotion that suddenly swamped him. He didn't know what to do with it. How to think past the raw surge of emotion charging through him. Justin had never been the kind of man to show what he was thinking, feeling. But this one tiny boy was changing all of that in a heartbeat.

Silence stretched out in the room, and he knew that he wasn't ready, not yet, to deal with Sadie and what she'd just thrown at him. It was as if the world he'd known only hours ago had been ripped out from beneath him. The ground he was standing on now felt wildly unstable. He had to think. Had to talk to someone. Straighten out his own thoughts and decide what the plan would be, going forward.

"He's a good-looking boy," he finally said, to no one in particular.

Sadie laughed a little. "Since he looks just like you?"

He shot her a look and, helpless to prevent it, smiled. "That did sound a little self-serving, didn't it?"

"It's true, though. I see you whenever I look at him."

Her voice was soft and quiet, as if she'd confessed something she obviously hadn't really wanted to say. And all he could say in return was, "I should have known about him."

"I can't change that now, Justin," she said, just as quietly. "But for what it's worth, I'm sorry."

He looked at her and wondered if she meant that or if she was only now regretting the lie that had kept Ethan from him. Either way, she was right. Nothing could change the past. Nothing could give him the memories he might have had of his son being born and the first months of his life. All they could do now was chart a course from this point.

Justin hadn't held a baby since his sister Serena's daughter, Alli, was small. Funny how it came back and felt…natural. But there was a lot to think about, before he allowed himself to talk to Sadie about what the future would hold. All he knew for sure was that he had a son and now more reason than ever to succeed. To bring his plans and ideas to life.

First, though, he needed time to think. Needed to set things straight in his own mind and get some damn advice—from someone he trusted—about what to do from here. Handing the baby to his mother, he watched the two of them together and saw the love shining between them like a damn beacon.

Suddenly, he was both father and outsider and

he didn't know how he was feeling about being either of those.

"I've got to go."

"Go?" Sadie repeated, staring at him in surprise. "Are you serious? You're going to leave now?"

"You dropped this on me, Sadie." His gaze flicked to Ethan briefly before meeting Sadie's again. "I'm going to need more than ten minutes to figure out—"

"What? What is there to figure out? We have a baby."

A son who would depend on both of his parents. Depend on them to get along. To work together for him. And right now, Justin was so angry with Sadie he could hardly speak to her. It was more than anger, though, he admitted silently. What he'd felt for her a year and a half ago had been seeping into him since his return to San Diego. And now, it was as if an invisible wall inside him had crumbled, allowing the feelings he'd been running from for so long, to come crashing back.

"What I need to figure out," Justin told her, "is what I'm going to do about it."

Four

After Justin left—she couldn't believe he'd left again—his features grim and tight, Sadie picked up her phone and hit the speed dial. When her mother answered, Sadie let out the breath she'd been holding.

"Hi, Mom," she said, swinging her hair back over her shoulder and smiling at her son. "I told him. I told Justin about the baby."

"Oh, honey. How did it go?"

"Just like you told me it would," she admitted and wondered if, as Ethan grew, she would become all-knowing, like her mother. "He was furious. Then stunned. Then he saw Ethan and the fury came back."

Her mother sighed softly. "He's bound to be angry, sweetie. You hid his son from him."

"*Hid* is a strong word."

"Have a better one?"

"Not off the top of my head, no." Sadie carried Ethan to the French doors leading to a small balcony and stepped outside. As she held him close and welcomed the cold rush of wind, Ethan laughed.

"What was I supposed to do, Mom? Go running to the man who walked away and say, 'Oh, by the way, I'm pregnant and you're the father'?"

"Well…"

"No, I couldn't do that." It had been humiliating, having him walk away from *her*. What if he'd walked away from Ethan, too? Well, she would find out soon enough if that was his plan, wouldn't she? But even that wasn't the whole truth. If Justin had ignored her or told her to get lost despite being pregnant it would have hurt right down to her soul. Yet, it was a different possible reaction that had worried her so much, and her mother knew it. "Mom, he's a Carey. They have more money than God. If he wants Ethan, he can find a way to take him."

Sunlight, the scent of the sea and the icy cold wind combined to soothe her as they always had. And still she walked back into their suite, protecting Ethan from the cold air. She carried him into his room while her mother talked.

"He's your son, honey," she said. "No judge is going to take Ethan from you."

"If the judge is friends with the Careys, he

might." And that fear was the real reason she'd kept quiet about the baby. She put her mom on speaker so she could lay Ethan down and draw up his blanket. "Nap time, baby boy," she said and her son kicked his legs, waved his arms and in general told her he really wasn't in the mood.

Scooping up her phone, she closed Ethan's door and walked back to the balcony that would always call to her. Taking her mother off speaker, she said, "I had to tell him, even though I'm still worried about what will happen next. The last two months have been a nightmare, trying to keep Justin from finding out about the baby. And frankly, it's exhausting."

"I imagine," her mom said.

"We're going to be working together and we're both living at the hotel for now, so sooner or later, Justin would have discovered the truth on his own. Might as well take charge of it," Sadie grumbled. There had just been no way to keep Ethan a secret forever. She'd known that the moment she'd invited Justin to come back and bid on the hotel. "And as soon as I told him…he left. Again. And he's probably gone off to get one of the three-piece-suit lawyers his family keeps on staff. God, Mom," she whispered, "what if he does take Ethan from me?"

"We won't let him."

A small smile curved Sadie's mouth. Good to

have support even if her mother couldn't actually *keep* that promise.

"Honey, you're reaching out for things to worry about and they don't exist yet," her mother soothed. "So instead, why don't we change the subject and you tell me what the hotel looks like now?"

Sadie walked back inside, dropped into a blue, flower-spattered chair and curled her legs up beneath her. Oh, she hated to admit it, but she said, "It looks wonderful. He's doing all the things you and I and Daddy used to talk about doing. The rooms are decorated beautifully and he's added French doors to the suites with balconies. Makes a heck of a statement."

"Oh, wish I could see it."

"You'd love it," Sadie admitted, because she loved what had happened so far, too. Not for the first time, she wished her parents weren't in Arizona. But it was best for her father, so she would deal with it. "The building's being painted this weekend."

"What color?" Her mother asked eagerly, then less enthusiastically, "Not the same brick red, is it?"

"No." Justin was too smart for that, she conceded silently. Whatever issues she had with him, she could admit that he was on top of things. What he didn't know, he found out. What he wanted, he got. Which brought her back to remembering how he hadn't wanted her—and worrying about him deciding he wanted their son.

Instantly, Sadie pushed that concern aside and

went back to the subject at hand. "Justin has been 'researching' hotels along the coast and has decided that the 'coastal' color scheme was the way to go."

"Okay," her mother said, "I think I know what that means, but define it for me."

"It's going to be a bright white with navy blue trim and a lighter blue as an accent color on the posts along the porch and on those French doors."

Her mother sighed and Sadie knew she was picturing it all.

"He's still working on the treatment rooms—though those are almost finished and the new indoor pool is gorgeous."

Her mother clucked her tongue. "Why an indoor pool? The hotel's at the ocean's front door."

Sadie laughed because that had been her first reaction, as well. "Justin said there will be plenty of rich women coming to the spa that aren't going to want salt water in their hair."

"But chlorine's okay?" her mother asked.

"I suppose. He wanted a couple of hot tubs, as well, but I talked him into going for a swim spa instead."

"And he went for it?"

"He did." Sadie remembered being surprised at how open he was to her ideas.

"Sounds like it's going to be beautiful."

"It is, Mom. I just wish it wasn't Justin doing it all."

Her mother sighed and Sadie winced.

"Honey, I know you don't want to hear this," she said patiently, "but this is happening because he's a Carey. He's got the money to give you that cash buyout and still pull the hotel into the twenty-first century."

Sadie knew all of that was true. She hated that it was true. Hated that she needed Justin as much as she wanted him. Just as she knew she'd needed that cash payment to send to her parents. "How's Daddy?"

"He's better." She could hear the smile in her mother's voice. "Much better, actually. He started arguing with the doctor yesterday, so that's a good sign."

Sadie grinned. "That *is* a good sign. So his heart will be all right now?"

"It will. He's on medication and since he's traded in worrying about the hotel for driving a golf cart, his blood pressure has really dropped."

"Okay, good." Relief swamped her. She hated that her parents were now living in Arizona, so far away, but if it meant that her father stayed healthy and worry-free, then she could live with it. Arizona wasn't a bad drive from San Diego, so she would be driving out for visits all the time.

Once this situation with Justin was resolved or ended or escalated, or whatever was going to happen.

So this was what she had to do, Sadie told herself.

She had to remember that entering this partnership with Justin—telling him about Ethan and handling that fallout—was for her father's sake.

When Max Harris had a heart attack, it had been a giant wakeup call for Sadie. Her father had been running and working and worrying over the hotel all his life and it was time for him to take it easy. Especially since the doctor had said that the heart attack was a small warning sign.

It hadn't been easy, but Sadie and her mother had finally convinced Max that retiring to Arizona was the right call. His brother lived there and Bullhead City had the Colorado River, so it wasn't just a desert landscape. He'd fought it every step of the way, but now, three months in, he was making friends, golfing a few times a week with his older brother and, in general, enjoying his life. Which made it possible for Sadie's mother to enjoy herself, too.

All it had taken was for Sadie to call Justin, swallow her pride and make a deal.

"Now, enough about us," her mother said. "Tell me everything new about my grandson."

Sadie grinned and settled in to talk about her favorite subject.

Justin drove like a bat out of hell.

The traffic on the freeway didn't slow him down any; it was more like the other cars were forming an obstacle course. He switched lanes, passed, switched again and stepped on it. He had to talk to the family. To Bennett. Hell, he had to talk to *somebody*.

He was a father and he didn't have the slightest clue what to do about that. The memory of holding his son rose up in his mind, then lodged in his throat, a hot ball of emotion that confused him. Hell, he'd been a father for an hour and his whole world was undone.

"Damn it," he muttered, "this was *not* in the plan."

Marriage and family had always been in the back of his mind, but somewhere in a very nebulous future, shrouded in mist. He hadn't been looking for a relationship, let alone a *family*. There was too much to be done. Too much left to prove. To both himself and the rest of the Careys.

But it seemed he didn't have a choice anymore. Ready for it or not, he had a son.

"Why didn't she tell me?" He fumed at that thought and passed a Camry like it was standing still. "The kid is six months old and I knew nothing about it?"

What would you have done if you'd known?

Well, he didn't know the answer to that, did he? He hadn't been given the opportunity to find out.

He punched in Bennett's number and waited impatiently while his brother's phone rang.

"Justin? Twice in one day? What's going on?"

"I've got to talk to you," Justin practically shouted to be heard over the roar of the wind racing past his BMW convertible. "Are you at the office?"

"No. I went home early."

"A very strange day," Justin muttered. His big brother leaving the office early. The world really was upside down. "I'll be there in a half hour."

"What's this about?"

"You won't believe me." Justin hung up before he could blurt out the truth. He wanted to do that in person and on his feet, so he could pace off the temper still chewing on his insides.

When he reached Bennett's house in Dana Point, Justin was stunned for the second time that day. He'd never much cared for Bennett's place. It was, he supposed, an architectural statement, but for him, it had always looked like a concrete box. But since Hannah had come into his brother's life, it looked like more had changed than just Bennett's attitude.

The building was still the same, but Hannah and her crew had done all they could to add some interest, some texture to the place. There were dark green shutters at the windows, window boxes filled with brightly colored summer flowers tumbling from them, and a new, gabled roof with cedar shingles over a wide, brand-new front porch that boasted gliders, chairs and tables alongside more potted flowers. The house itself was painted a softer green than the shutters, but nothing pale or ordinary. It reminded Justin of the color of moss when the sun shone on it. All in all, it looked a hell of a lot better than it had.

He climbed out of his car, took a breath, then headed across the flower-lined drive to the front door.

It swung open as he approached and Bennet was standing there, wearing blue jeans, a red crew shirt and black boots. "You wearing jeans?" Justin shook his head and walked past his brother into the house. "Don't know if I can take one more surprise today."

"I've worn jeans before," Bennett argued and shut the door. "What's going on with you?" he asked as he followed Justin into the great room.

"It's different in here, too," Justin muttered, shaking his head.

Bennett looked around at the deep green walls, the white crown molding and the gleaming wood floors, that somehow looked brighter now than they had when the walls were beige. "Yeah. Hannah and Mom are turning the place upside down."

"Beats beige, I guess," Justin said as he walked to the wide hearth, where he leaned his forearm on the heavy oak mantel.

"What the hell is wrong with beige, anyway?" Bennett murmured, then joined his brother. "You want to tell me what's happening now? Are you okay?"

"No." Justin took a deep breath, hoping it would steady him. "Nope. I'm really not."

"Just tell me. What kind of trouble are you in?"

Barking out a laugh, Justin said, "Thanks for the vote of confidence. Although, maybe it is trouble. That's the problem. I just don't know."

"Spit it out, Justin. I'm going to die an old man, watching you talk to yourself."

"Okay, then." Justin turned to face his brother. "Turns out I'm a father."

"What?"

"This is going to take a while," Justin said, dropping into one of the maroon leather chairs. "Can I have a beer?"

Bennett stared at him for a long moment or two. "I think we're both going to need one."

Sadie didn't know what she'd expected, but somehow it hadn't been Justin taking off the minute he found out about Ethan. She shouldn't have been surprised, though. He'd disappeared once before. Why not now?

If only she didn't still want him every bit as much as she once had. Those two weeks with him had been the best in her life. She'd fallen in love—that she hadn't expected—and when he left, her heart had shattered.

Until she'd discovered she was pregnant.

That had been like a gift. A miracle.

Sadie smiled, remembering, as she walked into one of the new treatment rooms at the hotel and stopped just over the threshold to admire it. Justin had taken what used to be small but tidy hotel rooms and turned the whole row of them into treatment rooms for the new spa. Aromatherapy, massage therapy, manicures and pedicures, exfoliation wraps…and so much more. It was going to be lush and beautiful.

In this room the walls were a soft meadow green, with sparkling white trim and soft lighting. Windows stood open to the ocean view now, but there were shades that could be drawn if the client preferred darkness. A small refrigerator would hold fruit juices and spring water. There were speakers on the wall to provide soothing music, and a dozen candles to fill the space with the scent of lavender or chamomile. Feather-light blankets and pillows that would soothe clients into sleep were stacked on a top-of-the-line massage table.

It was, in short, perfect.

"Boy, I hate to admit that," she murmured. Justin, with all of that Carey money at his disposal, was doing to the hotel all the things she'd dreamed of doing. So she was both pleased and irritated. An uncomfortable jumble of emotions.

"Oh, hi, Sadie."

She turned to the man in the doorway behind

her. "Hello, Sam." She gave him a smile. "I was just checking out the treatment rooms."

He took a long, approving look around. "Turned out nice, didn't it?"

"They all did." She surveyed the room again and gave a satisfied sigh. "And I love that every room is just a little different."

"That was your idea, wasn't it?" he asked.

"Yes," she admitted. "Justin wanted them all to be the same so there was continuity." She glanced at the lovely furnishings and said, "But I thought that having them be different, each of them luxurious in its own way, would encourage our clients to want to try every one of them."

She'd fought Justin on that and it wasn't the only argument they'd had over style. Well, Justin was a man and, sexist or not, most of their clients would be women. Not only was Sadie female, but she'd studied interior design in college. Plus, for years, she'd dreamed and planned and fantasized about what she would do to the hotel if she ever had the chance and the money.

Over the years, she had done what she could. But usually, the money she and her parents had been able to come up with had gone to repairs that really didn't show. New stoves in the restaurant. New elevator. New plumbing. Now, having the opportunity to do what she'd always longed to do, she was eager to do the rest. Even if that did mean accepting a partnership with Justin Carey.

"I think your idea was the better way." Sam shrugged. "I think my favorite is the dark green room. Makes me think of a forest."

"I like the blue one for the ocean," she confessed, then smiled again. "And we're proving my point, aren't we?"

"Guess we are. Have you seen Justin?" he asked and Sadie immediately tensed.

"No. He left a couple of hours ago." And that worried her. Minutes after meeting his son, Justin had left. Did that mean he wasn't coming back? No. She'd seen the look in his eyes while he held Ethan and it was enough to tell her that whatever else was going on in his mind, Justin wasn't walking away from their son. Which worried her in another way.

She wanted Ethan to know his father, of course. Of course. Her mind niggled at the wildly different scenarios that could play out and she wanted to reel back from all of them.

Truthfully, she didn't want to share Ethan. Not with a man who could pick up and walk away so easily. How could she trust Justin to *not* leave Ethan? To not hurt him as he had devastated her when he turned away from her fifteen months ago? But she didn't have a choice, did she? Because of the son they shared, she and Justin would be linked forever.

And the way she felt about the man was going to make that more and more difficult.

But that wasn't all of it. With the Carey family money and influence, Justin could, if he decided to, come in and find a way to take Ethan from her. And she couldn't risk that. What mother would? God it seriously felt as if her head might explode.

"Well, hell," Sam said. "Do you know when he'll be back?"

"No, I don't. Why?" Sadie asked. "Is there a problem?"

"Not really a problem. Just something I needed to talk to him about."

"Tell me."

Sam gathered his long blond hair and tied it off with a leather strip at the back of his neck. "You know they've been working on the indoor pool for a couple weeks now."

"Oh, yes." She and Justin had gone back and forth over the pool and the placement of it. Of course, at the end, Justin had won that round.

"Well, we're putting in a spa separate from the pool."

"Yeah, I know that, too," she said and followed Sam as he headed out into the hall. "I won that battle with Justin. He'd wanted a pair of hot tubs on either end of the pool."

"Well, we've got that swim spa you ordered all set up."

"Already? That's great." The swim spa was pool and spa combined and Sadie was sure it would be a big hit with their clients. It could seat up to twenty people, and had more than sixty jets. There were lights and Bluetooth for music and it could also be used for swimming against a current caused by heavy-duty jets.

"We're building the cedar decking and stairs now. Then we'll fill the spa. I was wondering if you wanted us to build a couple of cabinets you could use down there for towels and whatever else you might need."

"That's a terrific idea, Sam, thanks."

"No problem. The wet bar has two refrigerators, so you can have wine or your waters and whatever."

Sadie grinned. It was so much easier to talk to Sam. He actually *liked* her ideas.

"Anyway, I wanted to check with you and Justin to see if there were any last-minute changes you wanted to the decking around the swim spa."

"No, I loved the design you showed us."

"You think Justin's okay with it?"

She paused to think about it. "I think if Justin wanted a vote, he should have stuck around."

Sam rocked on his heels and bit back a small smile. "Power struggle?"

She shrugged. "Maybe a little." *A lot.* "Why don't you show me the spa setup?"

He led her through a door, across the courtyard

that also needed work, Sadie thought, to the building that was once used as a conference area. Well, with the emphasis now on building the Cliffside as a spa resort, they wouldn't be needing that space.

They walked inside and the cavernous room actually echoed with their footsteps. The new pool gleamed like a pale sapphire in the overhead lights. The new patio furniture was stacked at the back of the room and once they opened, this indoor pool room would be ready to help their clients relax and be waited on. Both sides of the rooms boasted floor-to-ceiling windows and the skylight overhead flooded the room with natural light.

"As you can see, the pool's completed. Finished filling it just this afternoon," Sam was saying as he pointed. "I thought the swim spa should be its own area." He turned to wave one hand at the opposite end of the room.

The swim spa, naked but for the casing it came wrapped in, sat, waiting to be filled and enjoyed. "I think it looks great there, Sam. When are you and the guys going to build the decking and stairs?"

"We're hauling in the cedar today, and we'll get started first thing in the morning. Shouldn't take more than a few hours."

"Perfect." Sadie's head was spinning. So much happening. So quickly. Was it too much? No, it was just happening so fast that she was having a hard time keeping up. She'd wanted to give the hotel a serious overhaul for years, and now that it was happening, she was both excited and irritated that she had Justin to thank for it.

The Cliffside was going to be reborn. And that was a very good thing. Meanwhile, she felt as if maybe her world was trembling on the edge of... something. She just wasn't sure what.

And she wouldn't know. Until Justin came back. *If* he came back.

When he did return, they had to have a talk. She and Justin were going to have to work together. They were both living in the hotel, so there was going to have to be communication. There was no reason they couldn't work well together, once they got past the initial bumps of being around each other again. And sharing Ethan.

Of course, she promised herself sternly, there would be absolutely *no* sex. Under any circumstances. They would not be going to bed together. That wouldn't solve anything and would only complicate *everything*.

Nope. Been there, done that, and not going back. No matter how good it sounded.

Five

Back in La Jolla, it took Justin about ten seconds to spot Sadie.

Sunset was over, but the moon hadn't risen yet, so the world was in that twilight stage where everything looked just a little softer. Streetlights were on, and small, white fairy lights were strung along the railing that ran the length of the hotel restaurant's outside patio.

But he wasn't interested in the atmosphere. He didn't give a damn about the pedestrians strolling along the shore or the music drifting to them from a group of kids gathered around a beach fire ring. All he cared about was Sadie.

She was sitting alone at a table far back from the boardwalk. She was in shadows and still he would have known her anywhere. Because there was a buzz in his bloodstream that only happened when he was close to Sadie.

Alone at the small round table in the soft glow of the pale lights, she looked…vulnerable. And she wouldn't thank him for thinking that.

He took a deep breath and released it, hoping to ease the knot of tension that had been with him since he'd left here a few hours ago. Talking to Bennett had helped—though it hadn't solved anything. He hadn't actually expected it to. What he'd really needed was just to talk to family. To get his brother's advice—which he wasn't sure he would follow anyway.

Bennett, after the first shock of finding out he had a nephew, had talked Justin down, made him swear to get a DNA test and had promised not to tell the rest of the family. Justin really didn't need the entire Carey clan descending on La Jolla to check out his son. Not before he had a chance to work this through with his son's mother. And who the hell knew how long that would take?

"Are you just going to stand there and look at me?"

His lips twitched. Sadie never had been the shy type. A man never had to wonder what she was thinking. Feeling. "I always liked looking at you, Sadie."

"And you always had something pretty to say."

Regret rose up inside him because of that tone of her voice. He didn't need to see her face to know she wasn't happy. And he really didn't like being the cause of her pain. Hell, all he'd ever wanted, from the moment he'd first met her, was to see her smile. To feel her touch. To taste that tempting mouth.

"I never lied to you, Sadie."

"I know." She dipped her head and her hair slid across her shoulders. "I think we should talk, Justin."

"Agreed." He walked closer, saw she was having a glass of wine and asked, "You have another one of those?"

"I do." There was a second glass on the table and as he walked closer, she poured pale gold wine into it. "I've been waiting for you."

Nodding, he took a seat beside her and asked, "Where's the baby?"

She took a sip and said, "Ethan is sleeping. Mike is with him."

"You seem to trust her with Ethan," he said.

"If I didn't trust her, she wouldn't be near my son." She took another sip of wine and said, "You're going to have to let that one go, Justin. Mike's a good person and she loves Ethan. He's safe with her."

"Fine." He lifted one hand as if in surrender. "I'll

take your word for it." *For now*, he told himself. He could have good ol' Mike checked out with a single phone call. He'd take care of that tomorrow. For tonight… "Anyway, I wanted to say that I'm sorry I left."

"Which time?"

"Nice shot." He slid a glance at her. "But is that really how you want to start this off?"

"No, it's not." Now Sadie lifted one hand and shook her head. "That was a knee-jerk response, sorry."

"Yeah, I guess we both do that too often."

"Probably," she said, then added, "I wasn't sure you'd come back."

"You can't be serious," he said. He sat up straight and leaned his forearms on the table. Cupping his palms around the wineglass, he spoke softly. "Not only are we remodeling this hotel and not finished yet—I just met my son. Why would I leave and not come back?"

"I don't know, Justin." Sadie sipped at her wine, pushed her hair back from her face and sighed a little. "For all I knew, meeting Ethan pushed you over the edge and you backed off."

"Not hardly," he muttered. "I just needed to clear my head."

"So, where did you go?"

This was the best conversation they'd had since he'd come back to San Diego. And he didn't buy for a second that she'd thought he wouldn't be coming back. Sadie was too smart for that. So maybe she'd just wanted him to explain where he'd gone. And why. Well, hell, he could give her that.

Nodding, Justin sat back in the chair, stretched his legs out in front of him and lifted the wineglass to take a drink. "I drove up to Orange County to talk to my brother."

"You told your family about Ethan?" Her voice was tight and her entire body went rigid. Tension radiated from her in thick waves and Justin wanted to know why.

"I told my *brother*. Why is that a problem for you?"

"I didn't say it was," Sadie countered, sipping at her wine again. "But why is it that the minute you find out about Ethan, you go off to your family?"

"Why wouldn't I?" He still didn't get it, though he could see that she was really off-balance about all of this. "They're my family. Who the hell else will I tell about Ethan? Why does this bother you so much?"

"It doesn't," she said, in a tone that shouted *Yes, it does!* Shaking her head, she said, "Why should I worry about you going to see the incredibly wealthy Carey family about *my* son?"

"So it'd be okay with you if my family had zero money."

"Yes. Maybe. This is coming out all wrong," she murmured.

A flicker of anger kindled in the center of his chest, but Justin deliberately ignored it. "Yes, it is. So you're trying to say you don't like my family because they're rich."

"I don't know if I like them or not. I've never met them. They could be totally nice people," she said, then took another sip of wine. "I just don't trust them because they're rich," she said.

"Wow. At least you're honest about it."

"Well, come on, Justin, when we were together before, you didn't exactly make me think your family was all Norman Rockwell or something. All you could talk about was how your family made you crazy."

"*Everybody's* family makes them crazy, Sadie. It's not just rich families. In fact, money has nothing to do with any of this."

"You know who says that? Rich people." Sadie rolled her eyes. "That and 'Money can't buy happiness.' You'll never hear someone living paycheck to paycheck say that."

"I suppose not," he had to admit. "That doesn't mean every guy with money is a jerk."

"I didn't say *every* rich person…"

"Didn't have to," Justin said with a half laugh. "The problem is, Sadie…you're a snob." He congratulated himself on his placid tone. "A reverse snob, but basically the same thing."

"That's ridiculous. I never—"

"Sadie," he said, still keeping his tone even—and good for him, "I wanted to talk to my brother. That's all." He shrugged and tucked his hands into his pockets. "If it makes you feel any better, he swore he wouldn't tell the family until I was ready."

"And when's that going to be?"

"I don't know." He shook his head. "You hit me with something that's going to take more than twelve hours to come to grips with."

She sighed, and most of the tension she'd been carrying around seemed to slide off her shoulders. Then she was quiet for another moment or two before muttering, "I'm not a snob."

He laughed shortly. "Fine. Leaving my family out of it for now, let's talk about the baby."

Her fingers tightened on the stem of her glass. "Okay. You start."

"I want time with him, Sadie," he said. That was the one clear thought he'd had all afternoon. "With Ethan. That's nonnegotiable."

"Nonnegotiable?" She took another drink of her wine before saying, "This isn't a contract, Justin."

"Not yet it's not."

She frowned so slightly that if he hadn't been watching her closely, he might have missed it. "We don't have to go to war over our son," he said quietly. "Look, Sadie. I've already lost six months of his life. I'm not going to lose any more."

"I don't want you to, Justin. That's why I finally

told you about Ethan." She set her wine down and quietly asked, "What did your brother say?"

"After he picked his jaw up off the floor, you mean?" He laughed shortly. "He told me to get a DNA test."

"He's your son, Justin," she said. "If you don't believe me, just look at him. He's a mini-you."

"I believe you and yeah, he does look like me. But for legal reasons, Bennett wants that DNA test."

"*What* legal reasons?"

"Nothing to worry about."

"People who say that never realize that those are the magic words that *start* the worry."

"Sounds like you're primed to worry no matter what I say."

"Maybe," she admitted. She leaned in toward him and he caught her scent on the air. Not cloying or heavy, it was softly floral and reminded him vaguely of peaches. And for the last year and a half, that scent had chased him through his dreams.

Justin looked at her, and in the glow of the white lights, her eyes shone as her gaze locked with his. She pulled the mass of her hair around to her left side and, as he watched, began to braid it, to contain it while the wind continued to swirl around them.

He reached out and caught her hand. His fingers burned at the contact with hers, and his voice was just a little tight when he said, "Don't tie your hair down. I like it loose."

Sadie ran her fingers through the loose braiding to undo it and kept her gaze fixed on him while she did. He couldn't look away from her. The night seemed to close in on them as it got darker, as if they were being closeted away from the rest of the world.

She took a deep breath, lifted her chin and said, "Okay. How are we going to handle this? I mean, Mike watches Ethan for me when I'm downstairs working with Sam or you or the others."

"That'll still work," Justin told her. "Or, sometimes I can take him with me while I talk to Sam or you."

"You want to take Ethan into the construction zone?"

"The heavy work is done now, Sadie. What's left is the finishing, the painting, the decorating."

"True. Okay, we can start off that way and see how it goes."

He took a drink, then smiled at her. "See, not so hard for us to talk without arguing."

Her lips curved briefly and he felt an answering tug inside him. This woman was burned into his blood. He'd never gotten past her. Never been able to forget her. And now she was here. Back in his life. With his *son*. He didn't know where that was going to lead them. Didn't know what was coming beyond the opening of the hotel that was going to be the first of many in the legacy chain Justin wanted to build.

All he really knew for sure was that he still wanted her.

The wind lifted her hair and Justin watched, hypnotized by the wild movement. Until she spoke again and he met her gaze. "Anything's possible, I suppose."

"Hope so," he said and reached out to cover her hand with his.

Her breath caught even as she slid her hand free of his touch. It was too late, of course, to prevent the sizzle and burn that simply touching her engendered. He took her hand again, yearning for that burn, and stroked her skin with his thumb, making both of them breathe faster.

"Justin," she said warily, "that's really not a good idea."

"I missed the feel of you, Sadie." He leaned closer, set his wine aside and looked into her eyes, enjoying the sparkle of those gold flecks. "We've been working together for nearly two months now, and you're all I can think about. Can you really say you haven't thought about...us?"

She licked her lips and almost killed him.

"Of course I've thought about it, Justin. But..."

"No buts, okay?" He stood up, then pulled her to her feet. Rubbing his hands up and down her arms, he said, "We're here. Together. Moon's starting to rise and the whole scene is too damn romantic to waste."

She looked up at him. "Romance? That's what you want to talk about now?"

"Who said anything about talking?" He smoothed his thumb over her bottom lip and she inhaled sharply. "Problem?" he asked.

"No," she said. "Just…kiss me, Ethan"

He did and she sank into him as if she'd been waiting for this moment for a lifetime.

She linked her arms around his neck and parted her lips for his tongue. At that first sweep of intimacy, she gasped and the sound set Justin's heartbeat galloping. For the last two months he'd been tortured every day with being around her and not being able to touch her. Tormented every night by dreams that were so real, so vivid he woke every morning in agony.

Now he had his hands on her at last. Was tasting her, at last. And all he could think was that it wasn't enough. He wanted—needed—more.

His hands fisted at her back and everything inside him did the same damn thing. God, he'd missed her. The taste of her. The feel of her, pressed up against him. The sigh of her breath, the whispered moans that slipped from her throat.

Everything about this woman pushed him to the edge of sanity. And she was the only one who could hold him there and make him enjoy the madness.

Her fingers stroked through his hair, tugged at the back of his neck, silently demanding more—

and he gave it to her. He held her tighter, closer, ran his hands up and down her back, following the line of her spine down to her butt, then he pulled her tightly to him so she could feel exactly what she was doing to him.

An instant later, she groaned, pulled her head back, and struggling for air, said, "This is a mistake, Justin."

"Doesn't feel like one," he murmured, dipping his head to run his lips and teeth and tongue up and down the line of her throat.

She tipped her head to one side, sighed and held on to his shoulders as if she were hanging off a cliff face. "It feels…amazing. But—"

"No buts, Sadie. Not now. Not tonight." He slid one hand from her back to her breast and she groaned. He tugged at her nipple, and even through the fabric of her shirt and bra, it was enough to jolt them both.

"That's cheating," she whispered.

"I'm just getting started," Justin told her, then pulled back. "But even if it is dark out here, I think we'd do better inside."

"Oh my god," she muttered, clearly horrified. She looked past him, past the shadowy outdoor patio to the boardwalk and the beach beyond. "I can't believe we almost…"

"Yeah, we've got an entire hotel at our disposal.

Let's pick a room." Justin took her hand in his and tugged her toward the entrance.

"What about the wine?"

"We'll get it in the morning."

She blew out a breath as she hurried to keep up with him. "Justin…"

"You're thinking," he said. "Cut it out."

She laughed and the sound of it rippled along his spine. "Justin, I didn't wait outside for you, hoping for…well, this."

"Too bad," he said, tugging her in his wake toward the elevator bank past the reception desk.

"I just wanted us to not fight anymore."

"Not planning on it." He punched the up button and waited impatiently, keeping a tight grip on her hand. When the elevator dinged and the doors slid open, he pulled her inside and had her against the wall while the doors slid closed again.

"Don't want to wait," he muttered as this time, he swept one hand up under the hem of her shirt, then under the silk of her bra to cup her breast in his hand. And the moment he touched her, she sighed and he was forced to bite back a groan.

"I've been thinking about this for the last two months," he admitted, burying his head in the crook of her neck. He inhaled that scent that was purely Sadie, and let himself drown in it.

"So have I, damn it," she said and arched into him as his fingers pulled at her hardened nipple.

"I didn't want to want you so much, but I simply couldn't help myself."

"If you think I'm going to feel bad hearing that," Justin said, pausing long enough to give her a wink, "you're wrong."

The elevator dinged again and the doors slid open. "My room," Justin said, cupping her face in his palms and kissing her with everything raging inside him.

When he lifted his head, she looked up at him and whispered, "Yes. Now."

Nodding, he grabbed her up, tossed her over his shoulder and grinned when she yelped in surprise. Then he was out of the elevator and striding down the hall toward the corner suite he'd claimed for himself. Black wall sconces that would soon be replaced by brass ones lit the way down the hall. Justin dug into his pocket for the key card, got the door open and when it closed behind him, he set Sadie on her feet and grinned into her smiling face.

"You're the only guy who's ever been able to just pick me up and walk off with me." She shook her hair back, then cupped his face between her palms. "I shouldn't admit how much I like it when you do that."

"I'll pretend I didn't hear it," he said as he pulled the hem of her T-shirt up and over her head to drop it on the floor. Then she reached out and did the same for him. The air in the room kissed his skin with a soft chill that did nothing to quiet the fires inside.

When she ran the flat of her hands over his chest, Justin sucked in a gulp of air and let it slide from his lungs on a sigh. Sadie flipped the front clasp of her bra and let it fall to the floor beside her shirt.

Justin smiled, set his hands at her hips and bent to take first one of her nipples, then the other into his mouth.

Sadie's back bowed as she moved against him. She speared her fingers through his hair and held him to her—an unnecessary move, Justin thought wildly. He wasn't about to stop.

He backed her up against the wall and feasted on her, sliding his hands down to the waistband of her shorts, undoing the zipper, the snap and then pushing them and the wisp of black silk beneath them down her amazing legs. She stepped out of her sandals and kicked off those shorts. Then he cupped her center and groaned at the jolt of heat.

"Justin!" Her short, neat nails dug into his back and he felt every tiny stab like a match flame.

His gaze locked on her face as he pushed one finger, then two, deep inside her body, stroking her incessantly as she twisted and writhed in his grip. He watched as those beautiful eyes of hers flashed with every emotion and sensation crowding through her. And when she came a moment later, he saw those eyes glaze over as she held him tightly and rocked her hips into his hand, riding the climax shuddering through her.

When the tremors stopped, Sadie slumped against him and he heard the shakiness in her voice when she said, "That was so good, Justin…"

He grinned, tipped up her chin so he could look into her eyes and said simply, "Just getting started, Sadie."

"I was hoping you'd say that," she admitted.

He smiled, swung her up into his arms and headed for the main bedroom in the two-room suite.

"I *can* walk, you know," she said, smiling.

"I like holding you," Justin told her.

Sadie wrapped her arms around his neck and asked, "What am I supposed to say to something like that?"

"You don't *have* to say anything. But…" His eyes met hers and he grinned. "How about *I love your manly muscles*?"

She laughed and Justin watched her eyes shine with humor. "Yes, that sounds just like something I'd say."

He laid her down on the bed, then stood back and stripped quickly.

"This time," she said as she lifted both arms to him, "I'm on the pill, so as long as you're healthy, too, we're covered."

He paused. "And is the pill a hundred percent effective?"

"I think it's more like ninety-eight percent," she admitted.

Justin scrubbed one hand over his face, swept his gaze up and down her body before settling on her gaze again. "I'll risk it."

"Me, too," she said, still holding her arms out to him in welcome. He moved into her arms, covered her body with his, and she wrapped her long legs around him, to keep him close.

Running her foot up and down his leg, she whispered, "It's been a long time, Justin."

"Fifteen months," he said and one corner of his mouth tipped up.

"Funny man." She slapped his shoulder and grinned at him. She ran her fingertips down his cheek and asked, "What're we doing, Justin?"

"What we do best, Sadie." He rolled, taking her with him until she lay stretched out on top of him and her gorgeous hair fell like a curtain on either side of their faces.

Staring into his eyes, she said, "Sex won't solve anything. Won't change anything."

"Does it have to?" he asked, running his hands up and down her body, following every line, every curve. "Why can't this just be what it is?"

Briefly, she closed her eyes and sighed softly. "What exactly is it, Justin?"

He looked up at her and smiled. "Magic, Sadie. Pure magic."

She didn't answer him and he tried to see what she was thinking by reading her eyes, but then she kissed him and he was surrounded by Sadie—her taste, her scent, the silken slide of her hair on his skin, the heat of her body soaking into his. When she moved, sitting up to straddle him, Justin's breath caught in his lungs. She looked like a goddess in the moonlight streaming through the windows. Her body was full and ripe and more beautiful than he remembered.

He reached up, covered her breasts with his hands and she covered his hands with her own. Tipping her head back, she shook her head and her glorious hair drifted from side to side like a sensuous curtain of silk. Looking at her, Justin's heartbeat hammered so loud it echoed in his mind. His mouth was dry and his throat clogged with a knot of need so huge he thought he might never draw an easy breath again.

"Magic," she whispered, and bracing her hands on his chest, Sadie lifted her hips and slowly lowered herself again, and as she did, she drew him into her body. The tight, wet heat of her had Justin gritting his teeth in a desperate attempt to control the need pounding through him. He looked up into her eyes and wondered how he'd gone so long without seeing her, being with her.

For those fifteen months they'd been apart, he'd thought of her often and had been tempted time and again to return to San Diego…to her. And he'd kept himself from surrendering to his want in favor of staying true to his plan.

Now he couldn't imagine why.

"You're thinking," Sadie said. "Cut it out."

He flashed her a grin, tightened his grip on her hips and held her still so he could savor that sensation of being deep inside her body. "Right. Not thinking."

She scooped her arms under her hair and then lifted them high, letting that glorious hair of hers slide over her skin, playing peekaboo with her breasts. While she watched him, she swiveled her hips, creating an amazing friction that pushed him further along the road to completion.

"You're driving me crazy, Sadie," he murmured and watched her smile blossom along with a shine of pleasure in her eyes.

Rocking her hips against him, she fought against the anchor of his hands and finally, he released her. Running his hands up and down her thighs, he listened to the rasp of her breathing, felt every move she made and gave himself up to the rush of sensations racing through him.

As a staggering climax came closer, he reached down to where their bodies joined and used his thumb to stroke and rub that one sensitive spot at the very heart of her. "Let go, Sadie. Just let go and fly…"

She reacted instantly, with a groan and a twist of

her hips, moving into his touch even as she moved on him, driving him on toward a climax that hung just out of reach.

"Justin!" She moved faster, harder, hips rocking while he matched the rhythm she set and lost himself in watching her. And still, he rubbed and stroked her core. "Don't stop," she whispered brokenly.

"Never," he answered on a groan.

She was amazing, he thought wildly, looking at her in the soft light pooling in through the open widows that faced the sea. Lithe and beautiful, she was the very definition of sex. And he couldn't imagine *not* wanting her.

She gasped, cried out his name and shuddered on top of him as her body erupted. He held her while she rode the wave of her release, and moments later, Justin leaped into that same abyss so that the two of them were locked together in a thundering, triumphant moment of completion.

When she slumped forward to lie across his chest, Justin wrapped his arms around her and rolled to his side, keeping her close so that they lay face to face on the pillows and he could watch every emotion that crossed her features.

"That was," she said, "really amazing."

He winked and grinned. "Thanks."

Laughing, she slapped lightly at his chest. "Fine. Take a bow. You earned it."

"Funny," he said, leaning in to taste that mouth of hers again, "I was going to say the same to you."

Sadie sighed. "This was never our problem. In a bed or on a table or against a wall, we were always great."

"Still are. Think we just proved that."

"But, Justin, sex isn't everything."

"Maybe not," he allowed, "but it's right up there at the top of the list."

"Justin…" She paused before admitting, "I promised myself that I wouldn't have sex with you again."

"Well, then," he mused, "you either lied to yourself, or can't be trusted with a promise."

"That's not funny."

"It's not the end of the world, either," Justin told her and cupped her face in his palm. "Hell, maybe it was a good thing."

"How do you figure that?"

"It sure got rid of some of the tension that's been humming between us for the last couple of months." He slid a hand down to cup her breast and stroke the tip of her nipple with his thumb.

She shivered, swallowed hard and said, "Justin, this morning we were shouting at each other. And tonight, we're doing…this?"

"Better than arguing, don't you agree?" He bent his head and tasted that nipple while he heard her gasp and sigh.

"Yes, but—"

He lifted his head, stared down at her and said, "Let's not question tonight, okay? Let's just accept it for what it is and be grateful for it."

Her eyes met his and he tried to read what was written in those golden eyes. She remained a mystery, though, and a part of him enjoyed that.

"Okay," Sadie finally said, then skimmed the tip of her finger across his chest, outlining the sculpted, tanned skin that she'd missed so much. "Tonight was…wonderful. But…I've got to get back to Ethan."

"Stay," Justin said. He covered her mouth with his, tangling his tongue with hers until neither of them could breathe. When he finally broke the kiss, he looked deeply into her eyes and smiled when she said, "I'll stay. For a while."

Six

Two hours later, Sadie was shaken. No other word for it.

She was still in love with Justin and that terrified her.

Nearly a year and a half ago, she'd whispered, "I love you," one night, and the next morning he was gone. The humiliation, the tears that followed had taught her a very valuable lesson. While the sex between them was, just as he said, *magical*, that was all there was. For him, anyway.

As for her, she couldn't seem to keep her heart from getting involved. And right now, her heart was racing and every single nerve in her body was buzzing. It had been that way from the first with Justin. He'd said it was magic and he wasn't wrong.

But that didn't change anything, did it?

She loved him.

He didn't love her.

"You're thinking again," Justin said. "Cut it out."

She laughed a little, as he'd meant her to, though her laugh had sounded strained to her. Then she looked at him and asked, "What do we do now, Justin?"

"About what? The hotel? Our son? More sex?"

"God." She stood up, pulled her shirt on over her head, then scooped her hair out and let it fall. "Just this morning, you were furious and now you're joking?"

He frowned up at her. "Would it make you feel better if we were screaming at each other?"

"No—of course not." But at least then, she'd know where she stood. As it was, the ground beneath her feet felt shaky. And if she lost her footing, it might cost her everything that mattered to her.

"Nothing's changed, Sadie." He crooked his arm behind his head. "I still want time with Ethan. Still want you. Still want the DNA test. Still want this hotel to be up and running in three weeks."

"And us?" she asked. "What do you want from *us*?"

"Well, now," he mused, his mouth in a slow curve, "that's a very good question."

She looked around the room, stalling for time. This room, like her own, was one of the few that hadn't yet been remodeled. All they really needed to do was paint, get a new bed in there, replace the bathroom counters and the shower and… Okay, there was a lot to do in both of their rooms. But there would be time for that later, wouldn't there? Once the hotel was open and guests were clamoring for space in a beautiful spa hotel with glorious views of the ocean.

Sadie had known for a long time that she couldn't continue to live at the hotel. Her son would need a yard. And friends. And room to run. She knew what it was to grow up living in a hotel, and though she'd had good times there and had made countless great memories, she wanted more for her son. She wanted him to have a tree house and a dog and—but this wasn't the time for those plans. Right now, she had to deal with Justin. How did *he* fit into those plans for the future? Heck, she didn't know if he would even want to be a part of them.

"It is a good question, Justin," she said, and gave in to impulse. Bending down, she planted a quick kiss on his lips, relished that quick, sharp buzz and said, "Let me know when you have an answer."

She made it to the door, and opened it before his voice stopped her. "What exactly do you want from me, Sadie?"

Looking over her shoulder at him, she said, "I'm not really sure."

* * *

By morning, Sadie had shoved the night before into a dark, dark corner of her mind. She hadn't slept, because whenever she closed her eyes, she saw Justin's smile. Felt his kiss. His touch.

And she couldn't focus on wants. It wasn't only her heart she had to protect. It was Ethan's. Loving Justin didn't mean that she was going to find a future with him. What it meant was that she was more vulnerable than ever. And she couldn't risk her son. If Ethan loved his father and that father left him, then what? No. Much better to wrap away what she was feeling and bury it deep inside her. Protect her son. Protect her own heart.

For now, what she had to do was work with Sam on the paint for the pool room and then talk to the designers working on the manicure-pedicure stations. She had some ideas on making the room the restful, warm, inviting place it should be.

Mostly, though, she had to go check on Ethan. Justin had picked him up early that morning and had planned to spend the day with their son. She'd been nervous ever since. Maybe Justin meant the very best, but Ethan was only six months old, which meant he needed naps and a bottle and to be changed and she was sure Justin wouldn't have the slightest clue what to do with a baby for hours at a time. Maybe she should have given him a schedule. Although, Justin probably wouldn't have paid any attention to it. He was too much the kind of guy to do things his own way.

But she also knew Justin would never admit when he couldn't handle something. So she had to find him and her son. She walked all over the hotel looking for him and finally found him out front, holding the baby close to his chest and pointing toward where the crew was painting. Leaning against a doorjamb, Sadie folded her arms over her chest and watched her son and his father.

"You see, Ethan?" Justin said, looking into his son's eyes as if expecting the baby to be taking all of this in. "If you need a job done, you always get the best people for it."

Of course, she thought, teaching their son how to hire people. The sun was pouring down around them and she smiled to herself to see that Justin had Ethan wearing his hat, to keep his baby-soft skin from burning. Ocean waves swept toward shore and sounded like the heartbeat of the world.

"But you can learn how to do some things for yourself," Justin was saying as Ethan slapped his palms together, applauding. "For example, your father happens to be a great painter." He grinned at the baby. "Not like an artist kind of painter, but I did help Sam paint his house a few months ago."

Ethan grabbed a fistful of his father's hair and yanked.

"Ow!" Justin winced and Sadie muffled a laugh

as she watched him trying to pry his son's fingers open. But he didn't get angry. Didn't lose patience. He looked a little out of his depth, sure, but he also looked…happy.

She should be glad to see that happiness, for her son's sake if nothing else, but instead, she was worried. If he enjoyed the time he spent with Ethan, he'd want more. He'd want custody. Maybe *full* custody. And she'd never be able to win a court battle with him. He could afford to hire a whole herd of lawyers and the only way she'd be able to do the same was if the hotel took off right away and started making profits.

She didn't have any spare cash lying around. Certainly not the kind she'd need to fight a custody battle against the Careys.

Sex last night had softened her up. Had smoothed off the hard, jagged edges of suspicion and hurt. Had he done it on purpose? Who knew? But the point was, it had worked. She'd smiled with him, laughed with him and shared intimacies with him that she'd sworn she wouldn't. Now Justin was clearly trying to ingratiate himself with their son while keeping her mollified with magical sex. She let her head drop against the wall behind her. God, she was an idiot. She'd stepped right back into the trap of loving Justin and having her heart walked on. Well, screw that. She wouldn't make this easy on him. No more sex. No more being soothed by his charm or sense of humor. She couldn't allow herself to let down her guard. Because the moment she did, she risked losing her son.

After all, Justin had walked away once before. If he did it again, he could take Ethan with him.

For the next week, they worked together to get the hotel ready, but it was as if Sadie had erected a wall between them. Justin hadn't been able to get past it. He had asked himself countless times if he really wanted to. The answer was, damn right he did.

That first night with her had whetted his appetite for what he'd only ever found with Sadie. Oh, he'd been with other women since walking away from her nearly a year and a half ago. But every time he felt a little buzz of interest for a woman, it had fizzled out before the evening was over.

Because she wasn't Sadie. And Sadie was always there for comparison. In his mind. In his dreams. Hell. Sometimes he thought that she'd imprinted herself on every cell in his body. She was so deep inside his soul, he'd had to run from her.

And the night they'd spent together a week ago had only awakened everything he'd spent the last year and a half trying to bury.

He wanted her.

Justin could admit that to himself without acknowledging anything else. Sadie hit him on levels no one else ever had and he was done pretending that wasn't true. And now, there was Ethan. That tiny boy was a link between them and Justin knew that link would be forever. So he and Sadie would have to find a way to make this work.

He checked the time on his phone and realized he had to leave or he'd never make the family meeting. Today was the day he'd tell the Careys about the Cliffside and what he was trying to build.

"Hey, Sam," he called out. "Have you seen Sadie?"

"Yeah. She's in the relaxation suite. Said she needed to make some changes."

"Seriously?" He shook his head, said, "Thanks," and headed for the treatment rooms. The relaxation room was something he had jokingly called the "recovery" room. It was set aside for clients coming out of treatments to take a few extra minutes to unwind, to savor a last little bit of pampering before leaving.

"And they're finished, so what's she changing?" The woman was driving him right over the edge. Not just physically, but in the fact that she challenged him on every decision regarding the hotel. It only made it worse when she was so often right.

He found her in the expansive room filled with comfortable chairs and chaises, soothing music piped in from overhead speakers and flowering plants on every surface. He spotted Sadie against the far corner, wielding a measuring tape like a sword.

"What're you doing?" he asked as he walked closer.

"Measuring." She glanced at him and then made notes on her phone.

"Sadie…" He wasn't in the mood for another battle.

"Fine." She glanced at him, then pulled the tape out again and laid it on the floor. "I'm measuring the space for the dual refrigerators I'm installing in here."

"*Two* refrigerators?" he repeated, stunned at the idea. "We talked about adding one," he said, realizing that a battle might happen after all. "And we decided that it wouldn't exactly fit with all the woo-woo relaxation stuff that's already in here."

"Woo-woo." She shook her head. "That's a pitiful statement. And no, Justin, *you* decided. I said you were wrong." She made another note and with a quick *zip*, the tape measure slid back into its case.

"Fine." Justin looked at her and waited until she turned to face him before asking, "Why is it we need a fridge—or two—in here?"

"Of the two of us," she asked, hitching one hip higher than the other, "which one has been to the most spas?"

His lips quirked. "If I said me, would you think less of me?"

"No." She grinned and shook her head. "But I wouldn't believe you. My point is, Justin, when women are relaxing, taking that extra half hour before they get dressed and get back on the freeway, they could use something to drink. Mainly I'm, thinking of flavored waters, juices, mineral water." She tapped one finger against her chin and spoke again, more to herself than to him. "We can have a barista of sorts stationed here, serving our clients, giving them that little taste of luxury. One more indulgence before returning to the real world."

He looked around the room, saw that she'd really poured herself into the decor. Pale lavender walls, gleaming oak floors scattered with rugs in jewel-toned colors. There were chaises and chairs and everything coming together to look exactly what it was. A sanctuary.

She'd been right about the colors. Right about the rugs. Right about a hell of a lot, though it cost him to admit it.

Scowling, he thought it was hard to take anyone's advice on this place. Justin had wanted this for so long, and he had planned to make all of the decisions. Make the calls on the look the hotel would offer. But he had to acknowledge that Sadie's input had been…invaluable. Whether he liked it or not.

He'd wanted to make his own statement. To break away from the Careys and build his future alone. Depending on no one but himself. But things had changed. He was building what he'd planned, but he wasn't doing it alone. The woman he'd once walked away from was now a huge part of the legacy he was creating and that fact wasn't easy to swallow.

Especially because somehow, she'd become… important. All over again. And he wasn't sure how he felt about that.

"Are you okay?"

Sadie's voice drew him up out of his thoughts. "What do you mean?"

"Well, I've called you three times." She shrugged and made another note on her phone. "Looked like you'd slipped into a fugue state."

Both eyebrows rose. That was embarrassing. "Well, I didn't. I was thinking."

"About how to get rid of the refrigerators?"

Reluctantly, he said, "No. More like I hate that you were right. Again."

She smiled, tipped her head to one side and studied him. "Well, that was honest anyway."

And she had no idea how much it had cost him to say that.

"Was there something you wanted when you came here? Or were you just checking up on me?"

He took a good, long look at her and his gaze sort of settled on the swell of her breasts even as he told himself to stop. When he lifted his gaze, he saw her narrowed eyes on him. Oh, yes, there was something he wanted. *Someone.* But he couldn't very well say that. Not after the distance between them over the last week.

"Yeah." He tucked his hands into his pockets. "Wanted to let you know I'm headed up to OC for a family meeting."

Her warm, whiskey-colored eyes instantly went cool and distant. Even though she was standing just a foot or so from him, she might as well have been across the room. Hell, he could feel the chill in the air around her.

"Great. Have a good time."

He choked out a laugh. "Yeah. It's always fun. Anyway. I'll be back later today."

She stared at him and he knew she was remembering, as he was, what had happened the last time he'd come back from Orange County. That one night of blistering hot sex had stayed with him every minute of the last week. Even now, that need hummed inside him and Justin fought down his own instinct to reach for her.

"I'll see you then," she said. "Drive safe."

When she turned away, he told himself to let it go. Once the hotel was up and running, they'd have to talk. About how they would work together. About Ethan. About what was still between them and what they were going to do about it.

Sadie didn't think about Justin while he was gone. Well, not more than four or five times an hour. But every time he popped into her head, she pushed him out again. Right now, he was going to talk to his family. And she had no doubt that this time, he'd tell them about Ethan. Because the hotel would be opening soon and they'd be coming down en masse to see the place—so they would naturally see Ethan.

Her nerves were jumping. Ethan was a Carey grandchild. That wasn't something Justin's family would ignore. So she had to be prepared for whatever was coming.

"And how do I do that?"

Ethan shrieked, slapped both hands on his high chair tray and grinned up at his mommy. Sadie's shoulders slumped, her heart melted and she smiled, helplessly. "You are the best thing that ever happened to me, baby boy."

He threw his head back and giggled as if to say, *I know that.*

Sadie filled a spoon with baby veggies and Ethan gobbled it down. As he played and crowed and laughed, Sadie's mind spun down all kinds of avenues. She had worked alongside Justin for a week now. And they'd done well enough together, though she had to fight to have her opinion heard. "But he does have the ability to admit when I'm right, too, so that says something."

Not enough, but something.

They shared a child.

They shared a bed—or had.

But they didn't share a life and she didn't see that happening, either.

And yet she loved him still. Couldn't change that, but she didn't have to let him know how she felt, either. That would only give him more power in their relationship than he already had.

There was no future with Justin beyond him being Ethan's father. She knew that. And she wasn't sure what he and his family might do about Ethan. So she couldn't risk letting her guard down. Couldn't chance believing this little interlude with him would last beyond the opening of the hotel.

"Hey, Sadie?"

She turned to face Mike standing in the open doorway. "What's up?"

"Your mom's on the hotel phone. Said she couldn't get through on your cell."

"What?" Sadie checked her cell and saw she'd forgotten to charge it. Fabulous. "Can you finish feeding Ethan for me?"

"Sure. Go ahead." As she left, Mike asked, "Is Justin coming back today?"

"He says he is," Sadie told her. "So we'll see."

"You really don't trust him, do you?"

Sadie stopped, and rubbed her hands up and down her arms as if fighting a chill. She wanted to say she did. But how could she? So instead, she smiled and said, "Don't let Ethan fight you on the veggies."

* * *

At the Carey Corporation building, Justin stalked through the halls. For the first time, he was looking forward to facing his family. Because for the first time, he was sure that he wasn't going to be facing a life behind one of these tinted windows.

It was a beautiful glass-and-chrome building in a pretty office park, with tidy greenbelts and views that showed off the 405 freeway and offered a smudge of blue that was the Pacific. He knew the Careys had done well here. Knew that this building was just a symbol for how successful his family had been over the years.

And he knew, deep in his soul, that he would never be closed off in this beautiful building. He was finally in a position to go his own way. Make his own mark. For years, his plans had built and grown and changed, but there'd been nothing solid to show for it. That wasn't true now, though. The hotel was real. The remodel was almost complete. And the Carey Cliffside was just the first of what he planned to be a chain of Carey Spas—so the worry about having to cave in to family and live his life their way was finally gone.

As long as the hotel was a success—and he knew it would be. Because it *had* to be.

"Justin." Bennett rushed up from behind and stopped him with a hand on the arm.

"Where'd you come from?" Justin looked around,

the long hall flanked by tinted windows and dozens of desks where employees busily ignored the Carey brothers. "I was just headed to your office."

"Yeah." Bennett scowled a little. "I was in Serena's office when I spotted you. Wanted to give you a heads-up."

"About what?" Suspicion colored his tone as his eyes narrowed on his older brother.

Bennett cringed uncomfortably. "They know about the baby."

"What? You said you wouldn't tell them." Justin gave another quick look around to make sure no one could overhear. But Bennett took his arm and drew him a bit farther along the hall.

"I didn't," he said, shoving one hand through his hair. "I told *Hannah*. Hannah told Mom. Mom told Amanda, Mandy told Serena and there you go. Chaos."

"That's perfect." Justin threw his hands up. "Just perfect. Thanks. What happened to keeping the baby news to yourself?"

"There's a rule about wives," Bennett muttered in disgust. "You're supposed to tell them this stuff."

"You're not married yet."

"Details," Bennett mumbled. "Besides. We're close enough."

"Isn't there a brothers' code, too?"

"I don't think so," Bennett told him. "And if there

were, it would lose to the wife code, I'm pretty sure. But is that really the point?"

"No," Justin said on a heavy sigh, then asked, "How'd they take it?"

"Are you kidding?" Bennett shook his head, shoved his hands into his pants pockets and said, "It was all I could do to keep Mom from hauling ass to San Diego to meet her new grandson."

"Oh, that would have been great." Justin walked three steps away and came back again. "Sadie would have loved that. She and I can't agree at all on what the future's going to be like, how to do this whole co-parenting thing… Yeah, Mom showing up out of the blue would be the frosting on this particular cake."

"Hey, I talked her out of it," Bennett said like a man looking for gratitude.

"Congratulations." Scowling, Justin grumbled, "Look, I don't even have the results of the DNA test back yet."

"But you took one," Bennett prodded.

"Yeah. One day last week," Justin muttered. "Mine and the baby's, and Sadie wasn't happy about that cheek swab, either."

"If she's worried about it, that's even more reason to take the damn test." Bennett tugged at the edges of his suit jacket, then buttoned it. While Justin watched, the new and improved Bennett turned himself back into the tightly wound Bennett that

Justin had known all his life. "What if she's lying to you about him?"

"She's not." Bringing Ethan's happy little face to his mind, Justin sighed as his heart seemed to double in size. "He looks just like me, Bennett. He's mine. I'm sure of it."

"Okay, say that's true," Bennett said quietly. "What're you going to do about it?"

"Be his father," Justin told him. "What else is there?"

"What about…I don't know…marrying his mother?"

Justin frowned. Nobody had even mentioned the word *marriage*. That wasn't on his radar at all. Not yet. The main reason he'd left Sadie a year and a half ago was because he'd known that she could be the one and he couldn't commit to anything more than the dream that was driving him.

Well, now that dream was closer than ever. He was on his way, but until he had his slice of the Carey Corporation stable and growing, he wasn't in a position to make promises to anyone. Not even the woman who haunted his every thought.

"If you don't want to marry her," Bennett said smoothly, "then I suggest you call the family lawyer. Make sure your rights as a father are covered."

Justin sighed and frowned into the distance. He really didn't want to bring lawyers into this. Not until he and Sadie had a chance to meet in the middle. To figure this tangled mess out themselves. "Since I found out about Ethan, she hasn't tried to keep me from being with Ethan."

"Not yet. But you're both living in the same hotel while you remodel, right?"

"Yeah." Instantly, memories of the night she'd gone to his room with him filled Justin's mind. He'd been aching for her ever since. And even living in the same damn hotel didn't guarantee that he'd have another night with her.

That thought was depressing as hell. He scrubbed both hands across his face, then looked at his brother.

"So what happens when you move out?" Bennett watched him, waiting. "Unless you plan on always living there."

"I haven't thought that far ahead," he admitted. "But the hotel will be open in another few weeks, and having room service twenty-four seven doesn't sound like a bad deal."

"Right." Bennett smirked. "And every kid deserves his own hotel hallway to play in."

Justin gave him a dirty look. "Hannah's been a bad influence on you. I don't remember this wise ass side of you."

"She's opened a lot of new doors for me." A soft, satisfied smile curved Bennett's mouth, and Justin found himself envying his brother's happiness.

"But my point is," Bennett said, coming back to the subject at hand, "kids grow up. Hell, look at

Alli. Jack's building her a castle in the backyard and they're looking at shelters for puppies."

Justin frowned to himself. His brother was right. When Ethan was a little older, things would change. He and Sadie would have to change, too.

"Sooner or later," Bennett added, "that kid's gonna need a house. Then what? You and Sadie live in separate wings and hand off the kid in the foyer every other week?"

Seriously, Justin's head was spinning. Not that living with Sadie, sharing a home with her sounded like a bad thing. It was just all coming at him so fast. He hadn't had time to think of any of this. "I've only known I'm a father for a week. Give me a break."

"You think Mom will?"

Not a chance, Justin thought.

Seven

With the hotel set to open in three weeks, there was a lot to do.

And with Justin in Orange County, saying God knew what to his family, Sadie buried herself in the work just to keep from driving herself insane with speculation. Her organizational skills were legendary and she was drawing on them heavily at the moment.

The courtyard of the Cliffside had always been a pretty spot. But since the remodel, it had taken a sharp turn toward Heavenly. The three-story hotel made a square as it surrounded the courtyard. Each hotel room boasted a balcony from whose iron railings hung lush ferns and flowering vines, which gave the building a lush feel that soothed the eye and scented the air.

Slowly, Sadie turned in a circle, studying the hotel's central courtyard. The flagstone patio had been pressure-washed and, like the front of the Cliffside, looked brand-new. For years, there had been massive terra cotta planters housing shade trees that dipped and swayed in the ocean breeze. Now, though, there were flowers at the base of the trees and tiny fairy lights strung in the branches. A fountain at the far end of the courtyard had been scrubbed and repainted, but the plumber still had to align new hoses and check the reclamation basin. She made a note to call him and confirm tomorrow's appointment.

Glass-topped tables with iron-backed chairs had been freshly painted a gleaming black, but the new cushions weren't in place yet. Stone planters stood empty, but tomorrow afternoon, the local nursery would be delivering the plants Sadie had ordered.

It was all perfect and yet somehow, she couldn't really enjoy it. Instead, she was thinking about Justin. Wondering where he was and more importantly, when he would be back.

"You don't look happy," Mike said, and Sadie heard the smile in her friend's voice.

"Happy enough," she allowed, then shrugged. "It's just there's still so much to do. And I haven't even started looking through the registration area to make sure the computers are online and—"

"I'll take care of that, Sadie," Mike said, and threw a glance at Ethan, who was blissfully chewing on a teddy bear.

With his playpen set up in the shade of the courtyard, Ethan was safe and happy, giving Sadie the time she needed to take care of business. "Okay, thanks, Mike," she said. "That would be great. Make notes of anything you see that has to be fixed before the opening."

"You got it. Uh, is your mom okay?" She winced a little. "When I spoke to her this morning, she sounded sort of…tense."

Sadie laughed, remembering her conversation with her mother. "That's a good word for it. Apparently, my father is feeling so much better he wants to buy a camper and hit the road."

"How fun!" Mike grinned. "So what does your mom not like about that idea?"

"Oh," Sadie said with a grin, "all of it. My mom's idea of camping is a two-star hotel. She doesn't do the great outdoors and now she's feeling pressured."

"Why?"

"Because she moved to Arizona with my dad to make sure he relaxed and took it easy. Well, he wants to relax on a really long road trip and she doesn't want to do it." Sadie completely understood how her mother was feeling.

After all, she had gone into business with the man she loved, even knowing that there wouldn't be a future for them. She'd risked custody of her son and her own heart—to ensure her son's future.

"Maybe they should get an RV instead of a camper," Mike mused. "More like camping in your house."

"And seriously expensive," Sadie pointed out.

"Yeah, but they could rent one first. See if they like it." She shrugged. "Worth a try."

Sadie thought about that for a minute. It might make a difference for her mom, and her father would seriously love driving a huge RV. "You're right. I'll suggest it and see what happens."

When Mike headed inside, Sadie was still smiling. At least her mom and dad were doing well. Dad's health was improving and mom was happy enough to be complaining about camping of all things. Which meant that no matter what else happened between Sadie and Justin, she'd done the right thing. She had to keep reminding herself of that.

Accepting his offer for the Cliffside, taking that cash payment, had made all the difference for her parents. If that deal had also made life more difficult for Sadie, it was still a price worth paying.

"Isn't that right, Ethan?" She leaned over the playpen to tickle her son's chubby chin. He laughed up at her and Sadie's heart soared. There was nothing she wouldn't do for Ethan.

"You and I are going to be just fine, sweetie," she promised. "You'll see. Now, chew on Teddy while Mommy goes over the nursery order. And every other thing on her list."

He flapped his arms, swinging Teddy in a wild arc. Sadie laughed and moved off to check her orders. Flipping through her phone, she went over the order from the local nursery. For the concrete planters, she'd ordered what gardeners liked to call *filler, thrillers and spillers.*

Thrillers were the tall plants, sure to catch the eye, and Sadie had ordered Tuscan Sun sunflowers. To be surrounded by sweet potato vines in a nearly fluorescent green as a filler and lobelia in a dark blue to spill over the edge of the planters. In others she had pink hydrangeas, blue lobelia and creeping Charlie ferns. The garden was going to be more beautiful than ever, from the fountains, to the flowerpots, to the arbor, where deep lavender clematis was already entwined. Everyone without an ocean view would step out onto their balconies to be greeted by the sound of dancing water in the fountain and a rainbow of color and scent.

It was going to be...well, she hated to use the word *magical* again, but it was the only word that truly fit.

Sadie made a quick phone call to the nursery and was reassured that everything was on schedule to be delivered the following day. She'd have plenty of help for the planting, since the hotel gardeners were eager to get back to work. With that thought in mind, she sent the head gardener, Tom, a text letting him know he should gather the troops for tomorrow.

There were still finishing touches to be done for some of the rooms and the restaurant kitchen was being set to rights by the chef. And the new menus were being printed. They had ads ready to run in California outlets up and down the coast, advertising the reopening of the Cliffside. "And fingers crossed, people will come."

They had to come, she thought. Justin had pinned his ambitions and dreams on the success of this hotel. But for Sadie, it was even more personal. More important. She needed this partnership with him to succeed because her son's future depended on it.

Yes, the Harris family had owned this hotel entirely, and for decades, it had supported them. But as bigger and more plush hotels grew up around them, business had fallen off. Their only hope had been a remodel her family couldn't afford. There were plans for bank loans and equity lines of credit, then her father got sick, and suddenly, there was no more time to waste.

Then along came Justin. He'd waved his millions at her, and this time, Sadie had gone for it. But holding on to that twenty-five percent ownership had been even more important to her than the cash payout she'd needed so badly. Her partnership would ensure her son's future, with or without his father.

"Sadie?"

She turned and smiled. "Hi, Sam." Then she noticed his expression. Fighting a sense of dread, asked, "What's wrong?"

"I just got off the phone with Kate."

Sam's fiancée, Kate O'Hara, was in the last two weeks of planning before her wedding and was probably on her last nerve by now. So if they'd had a fight, Sadie was ready to defend her friend's general crabbiness. "Is she okay?"

"Physically? Sure. Emotionally?" Sam shook his head, plowed one hand through his long blond hair and finished, "Hysterical."

Sadie took his hand, pulled him down to sit beside her on the iron chairs and said simply, "Tell me."

Justin looked around the conference room at his family. He was expecting to be ambushed by not only his mother, but his sisters, as well. According to Bennett, they all knew about Ethan. Yet, no one had said a word, and they simply watched him as he began to speak. And that was a little creepy. Knowing they knew. Knowing they were going to say something but not knowing what or when. So he hurried to tell them what he'd come to say before everything shifted to the subject of the son he didn't want to talk about yet.

"Well," he said, "I wanted to finally tell all of you what I've been doing down in San Diego."

"About time, too," his father, Martin, said, slapping one hand to the conference table, before leaning back in his chair.

"That's enough, Marty," his mother, Candace, warned. "Let's hear what Justin has to say." She paused, narrowed her gaze on Justin and added, "*All* of it."

He cleared his throat, looked away from his mother's accusatory glare and said, "I bought a hotel in La Jolla and I've been remodeling it into a luxury spa hotel."

"You what?" his father said, looking horrified.

Well, Justin hadn't expected anything less. The Carey Corporation was the Carey Center for the arts, the upscale Firewood shopping center and real estate holdings all over the state. If you didn't make your mark in one of those areas, Martin would not be happy.

Martin Carey was of the opinion that if his family wasn't part of the Carey Corporation, then whatever they were doing was wrong. But Justin was through trying to placate his dad or convince him of anything.

"It's a great place," he went on as if Martin hadn't spoken at all. His father was never going to be all right with this, so Justin was determined to convince everyone else that what he was doing was brilliant.

"Right on the beach. It's been there for sixty years and is practically an institution in La Jolla."

"An institution," Martin muttered.

Justin ignored him. "We've been working on it now for nearly three months—" He paused as he realized that he'd only just met his son at six months old. If Sadie had told him the truth sooner, he could have been spending the last three months getting to know his child. Funny that hadn't occurred to him before, but now that it had, he was angry all over again.

Even while he was *there* at the hotel, she'd kept up the lie, hiding Ethan, keeping Justin from discovering the truth. What the hell was the point of all of it anyway?

But the moment those thoughts crossed his mind, he had to acknowledge that part of this mess was his own fault. He was the one who had walked away. Why should she have trusted him to stay now?

"That's what you've been doing all this time?" He turned to see Amanda watching him, and was grateful to his sister for bringing him back to the subject at hand.

"Yeah." He nodded, brought images of the hotel up in his mind and said, "The rooms needed a lot of updating and we sectioned off a dozen of them to turn them into 'treatment' rooms…"

"Treatment," Martin mumbled, shaking his head.

Justin simply kept talking. He really wanted to

impress on the family how much he'd accomplished in a few months. How he'd set himself on the path toward the future *he* wanted for himself. "We've added an indoor pool and a swim spa—"

"What the hell is a swim spa?" Martin wanted to know.

"Marty, stop it," Candace said tightly.

Justin swallowed hard. "Every hotel room has a view of either the ocean or the courtyard. And both views are amazing. We've had crews working nearly round the clock for three months—" He looked at Bennett. "Remember how you had Hannah and her company working solid for four weeks to remodel The Carey?"

"Not likely to forget," Bennett mused. "It was because of the fire and the need to remodel that I met Hannah."

Justin nodded and saw similarities between himself and his older brother. The Carey restaurant fire had brought Hannah Yates into Bennett's life. And the Cliffside hotel had given Justin Sadie. "Well, I'm working with Sam Jonas— You remember Sam, don't you, Mom?"

"Of course I do," she said, waving that away. "Weren't the two of you thick as thieves for years? And I'll remind you that the whole family's attending his wedding in two weeks."

"Right," he mumbled, realizing that all of the Careys would be gathering at Sam's wedding, where they would definitely meet Sadie and Ethan and… he'd better well have a handle on what the hell was going on in his life before then.

He knew he cared for Sadie. He always had. But a year and a half ago, he'd left her because she was becoming too important to him. He'd had a mission to fulfill for his own sanity. To build his dreams apart from the family business.

And that hadn't changed. He was further along the road, but could he really give Sadie—and Ethan, for that matter—the kind of attention they deserved when he was so determined to forge a future for himself? And if he wasn't ready…was he willing to lose her? And his son?

God, his head was pounding suddenly and he needed peace to think. To figure things out.

But his mother wasn't finished speaking. "So what else is new in La Jolla?" she asked, with a knowing gleam in her eye.

"What else?" Martin looked at his wife, dumbfounded. "What? The fact that your son is starting up a business that's not part of the Carey Corporation isn't enough news?"

"Actually," Justin interrupted his father and avoided answering his mother. "Since Bennett invested in the hotel, you could say that technically, the Cliffside *is* part of the company. And I am changing its name to the Carey Cliffside, so…"

"Bennett?" Martin turned a hard stare on his

oldest son and Bennett shot Justin a look that said clearly, *Thanks a lot.*

"So you're in this, too?"

"It was a good investment and Justin paid the loan back as soon as the trust money came through."

"You used your *trust*?" Martin's outraged face turned an interesting shade of red.

"That's what it's for, Dad," Justin told him. "Besides, I didn't use it all, and once the hotel is open for business, it won't matter."

"Won't matter..." Martin's grumbles were drowned out by the raised voices of all the other Careys.

"And while we're on the subject, Dad," Bennett added, "Justin's told me that he plans to build a line of luxury spas up and down the California coast, to start. He says he's planning one in Newport Beach next. Eventually, he'll take the idea nationwide. And you should know, the Carey Corporation will be investing in him."

Justin grinned and Martin slapped one hand on the table. He looked at one son, then the other, hurt, the stamp of betrayal carved into his features. "Without discussing this with me?"

Bennett gave his father a patient smile and Justin mentally applauded. His older brother had found himself with Hannah. He was even more confident than he'd once been and that was really hard to believe.

"Yes, Dad," Bennett said quietly. "I'm the CEO now. I make the decisions for the Carey Corporation."

"And you just step over the old man to do it?"

Bennett shook his head. "Dad, you're supposed to be retired, remember? You passed the company on to us to take care of and grow. Just like your father did for you. It's our time, Dad."

Martin's mouth worked furiously, as if he were physically fighting to keep from saying what he'd have liked to. Justin had to give his dad points, too, for his hard-won control. Maybe Martin was finally coming to grips with his own retirement.

"When is the hotel opening and when can we see it?" Serena's question stopped him cold.

Justin didn't want the family trooping down to see the hotel ahead of time, because that meant they'd be seeing the baby and he wasn't ready for any of that yet. He needed to work things out with Sadie, and so far, Justin hadn't seen a way to make that happen.

"We're going to be opening in three weeks," he said, avoiding the rest of her question. "And actually, Serena, I'd like your opinion on some marketing ideas I've got. We have ads ready to go a week before the opening, in papers, online, in neighborhood magazines…" He laughed a little. "Hell, I've even got a billboard going up on Pacific Coast Highway, announcing the changes and the grand reopening."

Serena smiled and patted his hand. "It doesn't sound like you need my help at all, but I'm happy to listen."

"Thanks," he said.

"Does no one besides *me* care that Justin is stepping outside the family business?" Martin demanded, looking from one of them to the other.

"Apparently not, dear," Candace told her husband and smiled while he blustered. Then staring at Justin, she asked, "What about my grandson?"

"What *grandson*?" Martin shouted.

"His name is Ethan," Amanda said.

"Oh, man..." Bennett rubbed his forehead and Serena tugged at the sleeve of Justin's black leather jacket to get his attention. "Did you bring pictures?"

"He had better have pictures with him," his mother said.

No way out now. Hell, the minute Bennett told him that Hannah had spread the word to their mother, Justin had known that there'd be no holding Candace Carey back.

"His name is Ethan Harris and he's six months old." Justin pulled out his phone, called up photos and handed the phone to his mother.

"Oh my goodness." Candace immediately teared up and cooed at the pictures as she swiped through. Amanda and Serena jumped up to stand behind her and were muttering, "Slow down, Mom."

"*Your* son's last name is *Harris*?" Martin bellowed. "Now you're not even using the Carey name for your child? What the hell, Justin?"

Temper spiked, then subsided. He knew his dad. Martin felt cornered. Justin had left the family business; Martin's wife was living with Bennett and Hannah; and the old man thought he was slowly being edged out of the company he'd helped build. So Justin was willing to cut his father a little slack. For now.

"I didn't know about Ethan until about ten days ago," he admitted.

"Oh, Justin…" His mother looked up at him, disappointment and sympathy shining in her eyes.

He winced. "Now that I do know about him, things will change," he said. "Including his last name."

Since discovering Ethan, Justin had had that thought in his head. His son would carry *his* name, whether Sadie liked it or not. He didn't care if he had to officially adopt the boy he'd helped create.

"That's something, I guess," Martin muttered.

"And how are you going to get his mother to agree to that?" Bennett demanded.

"I haven't figured that out yet," Justin conceded.

"There's one very simple way," Amanda pointed out cheerfully. "We've already got three Carey siblings planning weddings. Why not make it all four of us?"

He shook his head. "Married?"

"Why not?" his mother asked. "You have a son. Do you have any feelings for his mother?"

"Of course I do—"

"Well, then?"

Damned if he'd be coerced into marriage by a mother looking to solidify a relationship with her grandson! Just because his brother and sisters were getting married, it didn't mean it was the right thing for him. He'd left Sadie once because she had been too important to him. Now, those feelings were even stronger. Back then, he'd had to focus on his future. On the goals and plans he'd set for himself. Now she was back in his life, with a son he already loved, and he had to ask himself if he was any more settled now than he had been then.

And the answer was no.

He couldn't risk a marriage when he didn't know if he was going to be successful or not. It had taken him a long time to figure out what he wanted to do in his life. And he hadn't proven himself yet. How could he risk Sadie's happiness and Ethan's safety? No. He had to make it. Had to succeed. Then and only then could he take a chance on marriage.

"I'm not talking about this here with all of you." He looked at each of them in turn. "That kind of decision is up to Sadie and me. I'm only here to tell you about the hotel and invite you all down to San Diego for the grand opening."

Bennett rolled his eyes and sat back in his chair.

Martin drummed his fingers against the tabletop while the three women continued to scroll through baby pictures. Justin noticed a single tear roll down his mother's cheek and knew that he was in deep trouble. Candace Carey was not going to be put off. She would want and expect to meet her grandson and she wouldn't be waiting for an invitation.

"If that's all the new business," Bennett said, rising.

"It's not," Martin said flatly and Bennett dropped back into his chair with a sigh.

"What time is it?" Bennett asked.

Serena looked at Justin's phone. "Almost noon."

"Where's your watch?" Justin asked him.

Bennett shrugged. "Hannah doesn't like it."

"This is too much," Martin announced to anyone willing to listen. "Too much is changing. Everyone's getting married. Bennett gave up his damned watch. Justin has a son. And a hotel." He shook his head as if waking up from a dream that was still clouding his thoughts. "My wife is living with our son and goes to lunch with a younger man."

"Really, Martin…" Candace frowned at him. "You're feeling sorry for yourself now."

"And who has a better right?" he argued. "Candy, it's time you moved back home and stopped this nonsense of living at Bennett's."

She handed the phone back to Justin and glanced

at her husband. "Are you ready, at last, to retire then?"

"I've told you I am retired."

"Then why are we at this meeting?" Her eyebrows lifted. "We should be on a cruise ship sailing our way toward England right about now."

Martin scowled. All four of his children held their breath and kept quiet.

"No answer to that, I see," Candace muttered.

"Damn it, Candy, we can go on a cruise anytime. Hannah's moved in with Bennett. Why don't you give them some privacy?"

She laughed and stood up. "So you want me home because you're worried about Bennett, is that it? Well, I can tell you that Hannah and I are having a wonderful time eliminating all shades of beige from Bennett's house."

"Wasn't that bad," Bennett muttered.

"Yes it was," Amanda and Serena said together.

Justin was just glad the focus was off him.

"Damn it, Candy…what happened to our life?" Martin stared down at his empty hands as if wondering how everything had slipped from his grasp. "I've got two sons going against me now…"

"Oh, Martin."

"You're only staying with Bennett to punish me," he added, "and now we've got a grandson who doesn't even carry our name." Shaking his head, he looked what he was. A man in his sixties, watching his family pull away and lead their own lives. The problem was, he didn't know what to do about it.

No one in the room looked comfortable with the turn the meeting had taken. But Candace stood, laid one hand on Martin's shoulder and said softly, "Marty, when you realize what's really important… you know where to find me."

Then she looked at Justin, and there were tears in her eyes when she said, "Your son is the image of you as a baby. Don't keep him from us."

Justin opened his mouth to say…something. But he was saved from stammering some half-assed reply when his mother turned on her heel and left the conference room. Amanda and Serena gave him their often seen, sometimes-brothers-are-just-idiots looks and followed.

Martin sat in his chair, staring at nothing. Bennett stood, gave his brother an elbow nudge, then nodded toward the door. Leaving their father in the quiet, they walked out, and Bennett didn't stop until they were far down the hall.

"You realize that Mom's not going to sit around waiting for you to bring your son for a visit."

Justin pushed one hand through his hair. He knew his mother. And more, he knew Sadie and was afraid that the way she felt about the Carey family, she wouldn't be happy if Candace showed up out of the blue and laid claim to her grandson. "I know."

"If it makes you feel any better," Bennett said

with a grin, "Hannah and I are doing our best to produce another Carey grandchild."

Justin laughed. "Work harder."

"I can promise to do that." Bennett slapped him on the back and said, "Come on. I'll buy you lunch before you head back. You can tell me all about the hotel and your son and the woman you're avoiding talking about."

"If I'm avoiding talking about her, which I'm not—" Lie. "—what makes you think I'll tell you about her?"

"Because you need to talk and I'm what you've got," Bennett said with a shrug as they headed toward the elevator.

Justin hated that his brother was right. But more, he was fascinated by the changes in the man that Hannah had wrought.

Their father was right, Justin decided. The Carey family was rewriting itself.

Would it turn out to be a comedy? Or a horror novel?

Eight

"Are you sure about this?"

"Absolutely," Sadie said, reaching out to give Sam a hug. They'd been talking for a couple of hours, going over and over everything, but Sadie had finally convinced him. Now Sam held on to her for a minute longer, and when he let her go, he was smiling.

"I seriously owe you for this, Sadie."

"No way. It's going to be fun." She opened up a new page on her phone notepad and said, "Let's get down to it. I love a good list, so we'll just write down everything we can think of right now and then add to it as we go."

"Did I miss something?"

Sadie and Sam both turned to look at Justin as he walked across the courtyard. She studied his face for some clue as to how the Carey family meeting had gone, but Justin's expression was deliberately neutral.

Which told her one thing. It hadn't gone well.

"Miss something?" Sam asked, shooting Sadie a quick glance. "Well, what you saw was a relieved celebration, but it really sort of depends on you agreeing."

"Agreeing to what?" Justin looked from him to Sadie and back again. Confusion sounded in his voice when he asked, "What's going on?"

"Kind of a long story," Sam said, "but I'll give you the Cliffs Notes version."

"Since I just got off the freeway, I appreciate it," Justin said.

"Kate called me this morning, crying," Sam said.

'What happened?" Justin stepped closer.

"Our wedding venue happened," Sam said and scrubbed one hand across his face. "You remember, Justin. I took you to that Victorian house in Old Town, San Diego?"

"Yeah," he said, "I remember. Kate found that place for you guys to get married in."

"Exactly." He glanced at Sadie. "She really loved the grounds for the reception and I didn't care where we got married, as long as we did."

Sadie grinned. "I love that."

"Right," Justin said. "So what's wrong?"

"Kate called me in tears this morning. A water heater blew out and flooded the whole place." Sam shook his head. "They're going to be closed for a month while the disaster crews come in to clean it all up."

"Oh man, that's terrible," Justin said, shoving both hands into his pockets. "How's Kate handling it?"

Sadie stared at him. "How do you think she's handling it? It's two weeks before her wedding."

Justin rubbed his forehead. "Yeah. Of course. Sorry."

"Anyway," Sam said. "The venue called her this morning and she's been crying ever since."

"Can't blame her," Sadie said.

"No, but I tried to help." Sam shrugged. "Told her it didn't matter where we got married and we could just get our families and go to the courthouse."

"Oh, Sam," Sadie muttered.

He sighed. "Yeah. That's when the screaming started."

"Okay, I get the disaster. What I still don't get is why you were celebrating when I got here."

"Because," Sam said, "as long as you go along with it, Sadie saved the day. And probably my life."

"Well, you are my friend, so I'd prefer you alive," Justin said. "What's the solution?"

"We hold the wedding here," Sadie told him. "Right here in the courtyard. We can set up tables and serve the reception from our restaurant."

"We're not open," Justin pointed out.

"Which is why this is perfect," Sadie argued.

"I really think she's right," Sam said.

"Your wedding's in two weeks." Justin looked at Sadie. "We can't be ready."

"Of course we can. We're mostly doing finish work now and all of the plants for the courtyard arrive tomorrow." She waved one hand at the wide, beautiful space. "This will be gorgeous. And it's not like we have to have treatment rooms ready. It's a wedding and a party. That's all."

"My crew will finish everything that needs doing in plenty of time," Sam said.

Sadie watched Justin and could see that he was considering every angle. So, to help push her idea over the finish line, she mused, "We can think of the wedding as a sort of trial run for the grand reopening."

He looked at her and after a long moment or two, smiled. "That's not bad."

"Thought you'd like that."

Sam grinned. "So we're good? I can call Kate and tell her we're saved?"

"Absolutely," Sadie said, her gaze locked with Justin's. "She can come check it out, see how she wants things set up—"

"Tell her everything's going to be great," Justin interrupted.

Sam shook Justin's hand, then turned and hugged Sadie again. "You might be sorry for this. Kate's mom is a little picky. But too late to back out now!"

As he moved off to call his fiancée, Sadie watched Justin. "He's really grateful."

"Yeah I can see that." He flicked a glance at his friend, who was laughing and talking on the phone. "It was a good idea to offer him this place."

"It'll be fun," she said, then changed the subject. She'd been worried since Justin had left for Orange County. She couldn't help it. Once the Careys knew about Ethan, everything might change. She had to be prepared. "So how'd the meeting go?" And did she want to know? Did he tell them all about Ethan? Were they calling lawyers?

Justin laughed shortly. "Like I expected. About the Cliffside, howling, shouting, my father acting like it's the end of the Carey family."

She blinked. Sadie couldn't imagine a family not standing behind one of their own. "Wow, that was a lot to throw at you."

"Dad's always had good aim, too," he said, dropping down on one of the iron chairs in the shade.

"Well, it's terrible. Were they all against you?"

He frowned a little. "Not really. Just my dad. Which I was expecting. He thinks the family's moving against him and it doesn't help that my mom is still living at Bennett's house."

"What? Why?"

"Long story," he said and thought about it for a second before adding, "Weird story. Very Carey."

Well, now she really wanted to know. Her curiosity must have been evident, because he said, "I'll tell you later."

"Okay..."

"Where's Ethan?" he asked.

"Right over there. In his playpen, sleeping."

Justin got up, walked over and simply stood there, staring down at the sleeping baby. And a niggle of worry sprouted in the pit of Sadie's stomach. His features were tight, his eyes shadowed, and he studied their son as if seeing him for the first time.

"What's going on, Justin?"

He shook his head. "Nothing."

"Clearly it's something, and if you don't tell me what it is, my brain is going to create all kinds of possibly apocalyptic scenarios."

He turned his head to look at her. "I don't remember you being this...nervous."

"I wasn't. Until I had Ethan." She glanced at her baby. "After, it's amazing how many scary situations my mind can conjure up. Everything from a tidal wave sweeping the hotel away to Ethan crawling off down the boardwalk and I don't notice until it's too late." She bit her bottom lip. "It's all about him now."

"Yeah," he muttered. "I get that."

"Hey, you two!" Sam strode up, took one look at them and asked, "Wait. Why the long faces? Did you change your minds? Because Kate and her mom will be here tomorrow going over everything. Kate's thrilled and grateful and cried again. The good kind of tears this time."

"Nope, no changing our minds. We're set." Justin slapped Sam on the back. "And don't worry. The wedding will be beautiful. We'll make sure of it."

"Thanks. Sincerely, thanks. Both of you." Sam nodded, tucked his phone into his pocket and said, "Now I'm heading to the third floor, to tell the guys to get a move on and finish everything just right. We've got a wedding to plan."

When he left, Sadie watched him go for a second before saying, "He's pretending it's all about Kate being happy, but Sam's really excited about getting married, too."

"Of course he is," Justin said. "Why else would he be doing it?"

Since he'd walked into the courtyard, she'd sensed the tension in Justin. Was it all over his father and the man's expectations being shattered? Or was there something else going on? She tipped her head to one side and looked at him. "Tell me what's happening, Justin."

"What do you mean?"

"You seem… I don't know. Not angry, but… something."

"I guess I am *something*." He ran one hand over the back of his neck. "The family knew all about Ethan when I got there."

"What?"

"Yeah. Bennett told Hannah, Hannah told Mom, and it was off and running."

"All of them?"

"Well," he said with a shrug, "all but my dad. He's sort of outside the loop these days."

"Oh, God." What did this mean for her? For Ethan? Yes, she knew the Careys were going to find out. Eventually. But it was here now and she didn't know what to do. Stay? Go to Arizona? Take an RV road trip with her parents?

"Come on, Sadie," he snapped as he read her expression, "they're my family. Are you expecting them to drive down here and kidnap Ethan?"

She wrapped her arms around her middle and held on tightly. "How do I know? I've never met your family." She shook her hair back from her face. "All I know about them is they have more money than I ever will and they gave you nothing but grief over wanting to live your own life."

Justin groaned.

"So why shouldn't I worry about them wanting to take Ethan from me and raise him as a Carey?"

"He's already a Carey," Justin said.

"His last name is Harris."

"For now," he said.

"See?" She jabbed her index finger at him. "It's that kind of statement that can push every button and nudge me right over the cliff of my own fears."

Turning his back on her, he walked away from the sleeping baby so they wouldn't wake him, and headed for the chairs under the shade. "Why shouldn't they know about my son?"

Instead of taking one of the chairs, he paced, then leaned back against the hip-high terra cotta pot. "And he *is* my son."

"Of course he is." She threw her hands up. "I told you that."

He stared at her, his blue eyes shadowed. "Yeah, but before I came back here, I stopped by the lab to get the DNA results. It's official. He's my son."

Amazed, Sadie shook her head. "Did you really think I was lying about Ethan?"

"No. Of course not. There would be no point, since it would be easily checked."

"Oh, thanks very much."

"And hell, he looks just like me. But somehow," he said, rubbing his forehead, "that report just smacked me in the face with it and I'm still off-balance."

Panic tangled with that small curl of worry, and between the two sensations, Sadie's stomach turned and her mouth went dry. "It doesn't change anything, Justin."

"Doesn't it?" A short laugh shot from his throat. "You know, I used to think I'd be a father someday, but when we first met, I was a bad bet for fatherhood."

"Justin…" She didn't know what to say to him. He was right. He'd left her the moment his plans evaporated. The moment she told him she loved him.

"I'm not sure I'm a good fatherhood bet *now*," he said, glancing to where his son slept. "But," he added as he stood up to face her, "I want you to know, I'm not running again. I'm not walking away. I'm sticking, Sadie. He's my son and I'm not going to lose him."

"What are you saying, Justin? Specifically."

"I'll let you know as soon as I have all the angles figured out."

"Right. Angles." Nodding, she turned to go to the baby, but Justin's hand on her arm stopped her. She looked down to where he held her, where the heat of his hand pooled into her body and sank deep into her soul. Then lifting her gaze to his, she said, "You want your son, Justin. Not your son's mother."

"You're wrong. I do want you."

"In bed."

"Is there something wrong with that?" He didn't let her go, as if he understood that she would bolt if he did. "It's been more than a week since we had sex, Sadie. Why're you keeping your distance from me?"

"I didn't hear you complaining."

"Maybe you weren't listening hard enough," he said. "So why?"

"Because I can't do it again, Justin." She turned her face up to the wide, blue sky that she could see through the canopy of the potted tree. "I can't hop in and out of your bed with the ease I did the first time we met. I'm a mom. I have more to think about than just what I want."

"So you *do* want me," he said, and one corner of his mouth lifted.

"Justin," she said on a sigh. "I'll probably still want you six months after I'm dead."

"Happy thought."

"We can't do this."

"We excel at this," he countered, stepping closer.

In the dappled shade of the tree, she looked up into his eyes and saw more than desire. She saw pain and worry and heat and so many damn things she imagined her own eyes must look the same. So why complicate things even more?

He slid his hand up her arm, over her shoulder, to the back of her neck. His fingers rubbed and stroked her skin until she was practically purring. "Justin…"

"One kiss," he said, "after a hard, long day. One damn kiss, Sadie."

He lowered his mouth to hers, and at the first

brush of his lips, she knew she was a goner. That spark of electricity that buzzed whenever he touched her. The slow burn inside that reminded her a bonfire was only moments away. The deep, throbbing ache that had settled low in her body and kept her awake every damn night hungering for him.

One kiss would never be enough.

And still, she wanted it.

She lifted her arms to encircle his neck and pressed herself into him as his mouth claimed hers in a tenderly desperate maneuver that had her trembling in his arms.

When he finally lifted his head and stared down into her eyes, Sadie knew they weren't finished. Not by a long shot.

"Tonight, Sadie," he urged. "I'll come to your room and once Ethan's asleep…"

She went hot and hungry in an instant. This would never change, she thought. She would always react this way to Justin.

"Tonight, Justin," she agreed and hoped she knew what she was doing.

Justin brought dinner—pizza and wine—when he went to Sadie's suite. It had been a crazy day, but things were starting to look up. It had been more than a week since he'd been with Sadie and he'd spent every night of that time half-awake and aching. That ended tonight.

He'd taken care of business with the family. He was on the verge of finally making his goals and dreams come true. Now it was time to stop thinking about a future that was any further away than the big hotel opening. All he wanted now was to focus on finishing this project, getting to know his son and enjoying Sadie.

He knocked on the door and when it swung open, he found Sadie, her long, luxurious hair in a messy ponytail and some kind of orange stain on her pale yellow shirt. Her mouth was tight, her eyes flashing, and there was a frazzled look on her face as she held a crying Ethan on her hip. "Good," she said. "You're here."

Quickly, she took the pizza from him, then said, "Your turn," as she eased the crying baby toward him. Ethan reached out both arms and leaned, still screaming, at his father.

"My turn?" he asked, taking Ethan and staring into a tiny face, red with fury. Tears pouring down his face, the baby shrieked, and it was like a nail being driven through Justin's temple. He looked at Sadie as she took the bottle of wine from his free hand. "What's wrong with him?"

"Well, that's a good question, isn't it?" She shook her head and that long ponytail of hers swung like a metronome behind her back. "Why don't you ask him?"

She carried the wine and pizza to the coffee table,

set the pizza down, then grabbed two glasses from a nearby wet bar before she dropped onto the sofa.

Why was she just sitting there? Why wasn't she helping? "What do you want me to do with him?"

She slanted him a look and there were dangerous glints in her eyes. "Settle him down. Give him a bath. Change him. Feed him. Put him to bed. Take him to Maui…dealer's choice."

"Sadie…"

She held up one hand for silence, then laid her head back, closed her eyes, and Justin was left to stare at his howling son in abject terror. Every other time he'd been around Ethan, the baby had been all smiles and sunshine. And his only other baby experience had been with his niece, Alli. Whenever she'd gone berserk, he'd simply handed her back to her mother and left.

Justin didn't think that was an option now.

While he was still asking himself what to do and how to do it, Ethan slapped both hands into his face and one small finger poked Justin in the eye. "Ow!"

"Yeah, watch those hands," Sadie warned a little late. "His fingernails need to be trimmed."

Justin looked over at her and saw Sadie opening the bottle of wine. "You're not going to help?"

She snorted. "Like I said. Your turn. You're Daddy… Have at it."

"Fine." How hard could it be? Was she expecting him to fail? Was this a test, somehow? Did she think he'd put Ethan down and walk away? He looked at his screaming son—the red eyes, the wide-open mouth, the flushed cheeks—and seriously considered doing just that.

But, Justin told himself, that would prove to her that he couldn't do it. That he would walk when things got tough. So, fine, he could do this.

She held a glass of wine, propped her feet on the coffee table and watched him. "Diapers are in his room," she said. "Food on the wet bar in here. Bathtub you should be able to locate."

"You think I can't?"

She smiled as she sipped. "I think you're mentally planning which route to take back to Orange County."

Yes, he was. But he would be keeping that to himself.

"Have some pizza," he told her and carried the screaming baby from the room.

"Good idea."

An hour later, Justin was exhausted and soaking wet, and he smelled bad, thanks to the ridiculously wet burp Ethan had dumped down the back of his father's shirt. But, he told himself as he eased out of the baby's room and pulled the door nearly closed, Ethan was clean, fed and currently asleep.

A miracle.

Stumbling back into the main room of the large suite, he found Sadie still on the couch, still sipping wine and watching him with an interested gleam in her eye. "How'd it go?"

"Funny," he said, sitting down beside her. He nipped her wineglass from her, took a long swallow and asked, "That was a test, right?"

"Yeah, it was." She smiled at him. "I wanted to see how you'd react to Ethan when he wasn't being adorable."

"Surprised I made it through?"

"Yes," she said, grinning. "I thought for sure you'd turn and run." Reaching for another wineglass, she filled it, then handed it to him and took back her own.

"Thanks," he muttered, then confessed, "I have to admit, running was my first instinct. Hand him off to you and get in the car. Drive. Fast."

"Congratulations," she said, lifting her wineglass in toast, "you are now officially a parent. We *all* do that. We *all* drive past a freeway on-ramp and think, *In three days, I could be thousands of miles from here.* But we don't go."

"You, too?" He sounded surprised.

Sadie laughed. "Of course me, too. I love him more than anything and sometimes, walking into the ocean and just keeping on walking seems like a solution."

"You know," he said companionably, "I never really gave my sister Serena enough credit. She was a single mom, too. Her bum of an ex left her—"

Sadie's eyebrows arched at that statement and immediately he knew what she was thinking. "Not the same. I didn't know about Ethan."

"True." Sadie nodded and gave a shrug. "Okay, I give you that. And now that you do know…"

"I'm still here, right?" Then he glanced at the baby's door. "Shouldn't we be more quiet?"

She laughed again. "No. Once Ethan's asleep, nothing wakes him up."

"Thank God." Justin took a long drink of wine. "How about some cold pizza?"

She studied him for a long minute and thought she'd never seen him look so…tempting. His hair was sticking up, the front of his shirt and jeans were wet, he smelled like stale formula and he was still keeping the eye Ethan had poked half-closed.

But, Sadie realized, he was more *real* to her in that moment than he'd ever been before. Her heart simply filled up and spilled over in her chest. She'd loved him before. Loved him still, and yet now, that love was suddenly richer, deeper and more terrifying than ever.

However, worry was for tomorrow. Or the next day. She wouldn't waste tonight.

"Cold pizza is always a good idea," she said. "But so is a hot shower followed by—"

He didn't even let her finish. "Sold." Justin leaned

in to kiss her and when wine sloshed over onto her shirt, she gasped at the cold damp.

He pulled back, grinned and said, "Looks like we could both use a shower."

"Conserving water," she mused. "Good for us. Good for the planet."

"There you go." He set their wineglasses on the table, then stood and held out one hand to her. She slipped her hand into his and he pulled her to her feet.

"Thought you were tired," she teased.

He looked down at her and gave her a smile. "I think I'm getting my second wind."

"Glad to hear it."

In the expansive and beautifully remodeled bathroom, there was a soaker tub in one corner and a massive shower with a bench and six different showerheads. Turquoise tiles shone under the lights and made it seem as if they were stepping into the sea.

"It's more than big enough for two," Sadie said.

"Best offer I've had in a long time." He reached for her, but Sadie slipped out of reach. Turning the water on hot, she watched steam rise while she quickly stripped out of her clothes. Stepping into the walk-in shower, Sadie stood beneath the rainfall stream, pushed her hair back from her face and watched Justin. Her heart galloped as he came toward her, and when he joined her in the shower, she reached for him.

"Whoa!" He jolted and hissed in a breath. "Is the water temperature set to *lava*?" he asked, laughing as he pulled her out of the direct stream of water.

"I like it hot."

"Yeah, I get that." He grabbed her and pulled her in close to him until their bodies were sliding against each other, and then he said, "Let's see how much hotter we can make it."

He tapped the body soap dispenser and then rubbed his soapy hands all over her body. Sadie closed her eyes and concentrated on the nearly hypnotic feel of Justin's hands moving over her skin. Up and down her back, over her hips, then tracing the line of her spine down to her butt. Then he slid his hands to the front where he caressed her breasts until she was breathless, then he slid those talented hands down her rib cage, over her abdomen, and slowly, lower. She parted her legs for him and when he touched her, stroked her, Sadie gasped and leaned back into him while the water pulsed down onto her.

Finally, finally, he took her back under the rainfall shower until the soap bubbles streamed down their bodies to the tiles beneath their feet. Then he flipped off the water, reached for a bath sheet and wrapped them both up in it. Roughly, he rubbed that thick cotton towel over her skin and his own until both of them were nearly vibrating with need.

"You're killing me," Sadie whispered while her body burned and her blood buzzed in her veins.

"Not yet," he promised, continuing to rub that thick, luxurious towel up and down her body.

"No. We're dry enough," she said and took his hand, leading him into her bedroom.

The emerald green duvet was tossed aside, and she pulled him down onto the crisp, cool sheets. When she would have hurried because the need was so huge, he caught her wrists in one hand and held her arms back and over her head.

"Not this time, Sadie," he said. "There's no rush here. Tonight, I want to savor you."

He trailed his mouth across her breasts, taking the time to nip and tease her hard nipples, suckling at her until she felt the pull of his mouth right down to her bones. She arched up into him, and whimpered a little, unable to swallow back the sound. He released her hands but still took his time, exploring every inch of her body as if he'd never touched her before.

And, she thought, he hadn't. Not like this. Not as if he were worshipping her. As if she were the most important thing in the world to him.

Helpless tears filled her eyes and she closed them, to keep him from seeing. But he was too busy to notice. He trailed his mouth down her ribs and across her belly to the juncture of her thighs, and Sadie gasped aloud. "Justin!"

"Savoring, Sadie..." he reminded her.

It was too much. Too much and not enough all at once. Her head dug back into the mattress as he parted her thighs and held her there. He dipped his head to her and his tongue and lips and teeth did things to her that drove her so far beyond pleasure she didn't know if she could ever find her way back.

Again and again, he drove her to peak, then pulled back, leaving her trembling, dangling from the edge of an abyss. Breath crashing in and out of her lungs, heart racing, Sadie choked out, "Justin! I can't take much more."

"Take it all, Sadie," he whispered, then slid up the length of her body until he was covering her. And as he kissed her, he slid his body into hers and she groaned because it felt so good. So right. So complete.

"I've missed you, Sadie," he whispered, burying his face in the curve of her neck.

"I missed you, too," she admitted and lifted her hips into him.

He pulled his head back and stared into her eyes. "I've missed you for a year and a half."

Her heart leaped and her breath caught in her throat. With his body buried deeply within hers, she didn't know how she was supposed to *think*.

"Justin…don't…" She said it brokenly, voice coming in gasps as he moved faster and faster, driving her toward the peaks he'd denied her only moments before.

He kissed her then, taking her sighs into him, cutting off whatever else he might have said. Instead, he devoted himself to pushing them both to the brink of madness, then, hands joined, bodies linked, they fell over the edge together.

Nine

When they could move again, Justin walked to the living room, grabbed the wine and pizza and carried it back to Sadie's bedroom.

She leaned back against the headboard and watched him, knowing she would never forget this image of him. Hair rumpled, cold pizza in one hand, with two wineglasses balanced on top of the box while he carried the bottle of wine in his free hand. Naked, his body was hard and muscled and tanned and made her mouth water, even though she'd just survived the most amazing orgasm she'd ever had. She wanted him again.

And always would.

He set the box on the duvet between them and she held the glasses while he poured the rest of the wine. He clinked his glass to hers, kissed her and asked, "Hungry?"

"Sure." Sadie took a sip of her wine to ease the knot lodged in her throat. Food wasn't high up on her list at the moment. She had too much going on in her mind for that. But she couldn't really confess that, could she?

He flipped open the lid on the box, but instead of helping himself, Justin turned to look at her and said, "Before we eat... I've been doing some thinking, Sadie, and there's something I want to talk to you about."

"What is it?" She held her breath, unsure where he was going and not at all sure she was going to like it.

"Well," he started, then paused to sip at his wine, "we both love Ethan—"

"Yes." And she loved Justin, but he wouldn't want to hear that, so she kept it to herself and waited.

He flipped on a bedside lamp and a small circle of golden light fell across the bed. "We're his parents, Sadie, so you know, between us, we have to find a way to do what's best for him."

Carefully, she set her wineglass on the bedside table and swallowed down the quick slash of fear that ripped through her. When she looked at him, she deliberately kept her voice calm.

"What's best for him?" she repeated. "In what way? The best schools, a fancy house, nice car when he's old enough? Just what are you talking about, Justin?"

"Why are you suddenly so hostile?" he asked. "I haven't said anything yet."

"I know what's coming," she said, "and I'm telling you right now, Justin. You can't take Ethan away from me and say it's for his own good."

"What are you talking about?" He pulled back, clearly surprised. "I didn't say that."

"You didn't have to," she countered. God, how could they have been so close moments ago and at odds now? She loved him and couldn't tell him. Couldn't let him know just how close to the edge she really was. He'd been with his family earlier today and now, she was terrified of what that might mean to her. To them. "Your family is involved now. They'll want their grandson being raised the 'right' way."

He choked out a laugh and shook his head. "The right way? What the hell, Sadie?"

She wasn't listening. Her fear was driving her words and she had to make her position clear to him right now. She wouldn't risk Ethan. "You'll try to take him because you can afford the best attorneys and I can't. But I'll fight anyway, Justin."

He pushed one hand through his hair. "Who are you going to fight? And where are you getting all of this in the first place? I'm not trying to take him away from you, Sadie." Setting his glass down, as well, he took both of her hands in his, met her gaze squarely and said, "When I said we could do what's best for him, I meant that we could get married."

For several heartbeats, she simply stared at him. As if she wasn't entirely sure she'd heard him correctly. But the way he was watching her, waiting, told her she had. Still, it made no sense.

"Married?" Her heart pounded in her chest.

"Exactly!" He beamed at her like a teacher proud of a student who had finally caught on to a confusing problem.

"When did you come up with this?"

"Well, Sam and Kate got me thinking about it, really."

"You're not making any sense, Justin." Her breath came in short, sharp gasps, but she didn't think he'd noticed at all. Sadie didn't know what to think, what to feel. So she listened and hoped for the best. Married?

"Give me a chance. I'm getting to it. We're hosting their wedding here—"

"Yeah?"

"They'll be married. Sharing everything. Living together."

"Well, yes, Justin. What's your point?"

He frowned, probably because he knew he wasn't getting his point across very well. "I just thought about it and realized that if we're married, Ethan has two parents and—"

"And?"

"And we'd be a team, Sadie. We're good together. You know that. We share a son." He blew out a breath and shook his head. "I don't know, I just think it would be best is all. For Ethan. And for us." He grinned at her, warming to his subject. "I know I'm not at my most convincing at the moment, but think about it, Sadie.

"Look, we've already proved these last few months that we work well together. Once the Carey Cliffside is open for business, we can get to work on the hotel in Newport Beach. And from there, wherever we want. We can transform hotels all over the state and do it as a team. You, me, Ethan. All three of us.

"Sadie, we like each other. We share Ethan. And damn it, we're *great* in bed. Why shouldn't we get married?"

And just like that, nerves and fear and hope collided in her chest and died miserable deaths. He was willing to marry her because it made things easier for him. Marriage itself didn't mean anything. He would get a partner at work, an eager bedmate and a son out of the deal. What wasn't to like?

But Sadie wasn't that desperate. That lonely. She loved Justin Carey. How could she marry him knowing that he didn't love her? How could she settle for a marriage that wasn't real? If she did that, her heart would slowly wither and die.

Reaching for her wine, she drained the glass, set it down again and turned to face the man watching her. The man she loved. The man she couldn't have.

"What do you say?" he asked, giving her the half smile that always showcased the dimple in his cheek. He was everything she wanted. And now she knew for sure that she'd never have him. Not the way she wanted. He offered her marriage, but he didn't love her. And knowing that, feeling that, hurt more than she could have imagined. But she wouldn't let him see that.

"Where do I start," she wondered aloud. "That was simply an *enchanting, romantic* proposal, Justin. Romantic enough that if I had a diary, I'd write it all down."

"Romantic?" He scowled at her. "Who's talking about romance?"

"Neither of us, as it turns out," she said quietly. "One day, I'll be sure to tell Ethan that his daddy loved him so much that he was willing to sacrifice himself on the altar of marriage."

"What the hell?" He pushed off the bed and stood facing her.

"You actually look surprised that I'm not happy about your idea of a proposal."

"No." He stopped and corrected himself. "Well,

yeah. I am. It's a great idea, Sadie. Why can't you see that?"

"What I can see is that you're still running. The only difference is, you haven't left."

"You're not making any sense."

"Right." She nodded and stood up. "It's *me*. Well, thanks for that generous offer, but I don't need a pity wedding ring—"

"Pity?" He shoved both hands through his hair as if he couldn't understand how he'd lost control of the whole situation.

"That's not what marriage is, Justin. My God, your parents have been together more than forty years—just like mine. Do you think they did it all because they made a good team? Or because they were great together in bed?"

He held up one hand. "I do not want to think about that."

She sighed. "My point is, marriage is about love. That's why Sam and Kate are getting married. That's why our parents are *still* married. Remember what I said to you our last night together before you left a year and a half ago?"

His features went blank and hard. "I remember and I know you didn't mean it." He shrugged. "It's just the kind of thing you say after great sex."

"Right. Because I've heard you say 'I love you' many times after great sex, so, good point." Shaking her head, Sadie said, "I told you I loved you and I

meant it, Justin. I loved you then. I love you now—
though I couldn't tell you why at the moment—so
no, I won't marry you. Because frankly, I deserve
better." She slipped a robe on, turned her back on
Justin and said, "I think you should go."

For a week, they were too busy to revisit that conversation even if they'd wanted to. Justin, Sam and
the crew focused on finishing up the small touches
left, while Sadie and Kate concentrated on turning
the courtyard into a "fairy garden" setting for the
wedding.

Kate was a nervous wreck, of course, but she simply radiated happiness that Sadie had a hard time
not envying. It wasn't as if she begrudged Kate her
happiness—she only wanted it for herself, as well.

But the odds of that happening with Justin were
now zero. He hadn't spoken to her except in the most
coolly polite terms since that night in her room. He
visited Ethan, played with him, took care of him,
but he had nothing to say to Sadie. It was as if they'd
said it all that last night together.

Sadie's heart ached. How she wished things were
different. She loved Justin and always would. If that
proposal had been a real one, she'd have accepted in
a dirty minute. Because he was right about at least
one thing. They did make a good team. But without
love, what was the point of marriage?

She took a breath, smiled and told herself, "It's going to be a gorgeous wedding."

"I think you're right."

Justin's voice. How had he slipped up behind her without her noticing? Because, Sadie thought, she'd been too busy wishing for what might have been.

"Kate loves all of this," he said, and she looked at the courtyard through a bride's eyes. Not only did they have the original plants that Sadie had ordered, but now there was an arbor covered with trailing, dark blue clematis. There were ornamental iron stands holding terra cotta pots filled with jewel-toned flowers. On either side of the aisle that Kate was to walk down were chairs that would, on the big day, be draped in pale green cloth, while pots of bright pink and white petunias lined the white silk runner. The ceremony would take place beneath the arbor, and once it was over, tables would be brought out for the feast prepared and catered by the hotel.

Sadie saw it all and realized that this was exactly what she would have wanted for her own wedding. A sort of casual sophistication.

"She's pretty happy about it all," Sadie said, still not turning to look at Justin. "Even her mother is pleased and loves the arbor. I'm glad Kate's going to have the wedding day she wanted."

"Yeah." He paused. "Well, Sam says she can't stop talking about all you've done. He's really grateful, Sadie." He touched her arm, turned her to face him. "You saved their wedding for them."

"We did," she said and avoided meeting his gaze.

"Yeah, we did." He tipped her chin up until she had no choice but to look at him. "I'm sorry I've been…quiet this last week."

"Have you?"

He smiled. "Fine. You didn't notice. Look, I don't like having my plans messed with, and you saying no threw me. Like I said. We make a great team."

She shook her head and bit her tongue. It was pointless to go over it all again. "Stop it, Justin. Just stop."

His hand on her arm tightened. "Why? You said you love me."

She looked up at him. "Yes, but I'll get over it."

He choked out a laugh. "You would, too. But what I'm saying is why try? If you love me, marry me. Good for you. Good for me. Good for Ethan."

"Don't you get it?" she asked. "A one-sided love is not a good time for the one doing the loving."

"Sadie…" He threw his hands up in frustration. "Damn it. You *matter* to me."

"Uh-huh. Your black leather jacket matters to you, too, Justin."

"Now you're being ridiculous."

"Am I?" She gathered up her long hair that was flying all over the place and did a quick braid that wouldn't last more than five minutes, since she didn't have anything to hold the ends, but she needed something to occupy her hands. "I don't think I am. I think we've run our course and one of us has to be the one to say it. Guess that's me."

"But you said you love me."

"Sadly," she said, staring up at him, "love doesn't solve everything."

"Damn it, Sadie." He tipped his head back, stared up at the cloud-studded sky briefly, then looked at her again. "Everything I've worked for the last few years is on the line right now. This hotel opening is it for me. Make it or break it. If it goes well, sky's the limit. If it doesn't…well. I'm not going to accept anything less than success. So don't you think there's a lot going on right now for us to be having these conversations?"

"Hey," she reminded him, "you're the one who gave me that tired, empty proposal. If you can't deal with my answer, then that's your problem."

Her eyes were stinging but she refused to cry. He couldn't see the truth because he didn't want to see it.

"It wasn't tired or empty," he told her flatly. "It was an offer to join me. To be my partner."

"If you want a business partner, you write a contract, not a marriage license." God, if her heart cracked one more time, it would simply shatter and tumble out of her chest.

"Now," she said sharply, "I really need to get

Ethan. It's his lunchtime and like his father, he gets crabby when he's hungry."

Sadie skirted around the rows of chairs and walked to where a playpen was set up in the shade. She knew Justin was right behind her, because she could feel a buzz in the air.

Why wouldn't he let this go? Why try so hard to get her to marry him if he didn't love her? Was it all for Ethan's sake? A way for him to have his son without taking him from her?

And if she didn't agree, would he move on to an expensive lawyer and sue for custody? But how could she marry him knowing that he didn't love her? Or wouldn't, which was basically the same thing. That kind of marriage would be empty and it would slowly, daily grind her heart into dust. And hell, eventually, even Ethan would notice.

"Don't you have something to do?" she asked, tossing the question over her shoulder.

"I'm doing it. I want to see my son. Go take a break or something," he offered. "I'll feed Ethan."

"It's okay. I don't need a break." Nice of him, she supposed, but she needed this time with Ethan. To remind herself of how much she already had in her life.

She smiled down at her son as he kicked his legs and waved his arms. He never failed to make her smile and today was no different.

She leaned over, scooped him up and gave him a

loud, smacking kiss that had Ethan giggling. That wonderful belly laugh was enough to remind her that life was pretty great. That she was a mom, with someone who depended on her. That it was up to *her* to make her life the way she wanted it.

She tucked Ethan onto her left hip and automatically started swaying as she reached down for his diaper bag.

"I'll get it," Justin said.

"Justin…" Before he could pick up the bag, Ethan laughed again and launched himself at his father. Sadie could only watch as Justin grabbed him, then swung him up in the air to make the tiny boy laugh himself silly.

Her heart ached to see them together. To know that they would never be the family she'd dreamed of.

Movement at the corner of her eye caught her attention and she said, "Someone's here. I guess they think we're open, what with all the activity."

Justin, still grinning, lowered Ethan to his chest and turned to look. Sadie watched his smile slowly dissolve. "That's my family. Well, some of them."

"What?" She looked at the three people walking toward them and saw that they were hurrying forward now. All Sadie could think was that her hair was a mess, she was dressed like a hobo and she was probably sweaty on top of it all. "Oh, God."

He grabbed her hand as if he thought she might

make a run for it—he was right. "Come on, Sadie," he muttered. "You're tougher than that."

He was right about that, too, damn it. Tugging her with him, he walked toward his family. "Mom," he said. "What are you doing here?"

"There he is," the older woman said eagerly, her gaze fixed on Ethan. "I couldn't stand it. Had to come and meet my grandson!"

Justin sighed and Sadie had to fight the urge to grab her son and get out of there. Instead, she listened while Justin made introductions.

"Well," the woman said with a wide smile, "I just couldn't wait until Sam's wedding to meet my grandson! So I talked Bennett and Hannah into coming with me."

"This wasn't my idea," Bennett pointed out.

Hannah gave him a hard elbow nudge.

"You're coming to the wedding?" Sadie asked.

"Oh, yes," Justin's mother said. "We've known Sam for years. Now, Justin, don't you think you should introduce us?"

He sighed a little and Sadie thought it sounded like a surrender.

"Mom, this is Sadie Harris. My partner in this hotel." That sounded sad, but he probably didn't think so. "Sadie, my mother, Candace Carey."

"Call me Candace," she said and spared a quick smile for Sadie. The woman was elegant. She wore a slate gray skirt and jacket with a deep scarlet blouse.

Her heels were the same shade of gray as her suit and her short brown hair was expertly styled with streaks of a dark red running through it.

Sadie felt even shabbier than before, in comparison. "It's nice to meet you."

"Oh, that's a nice thing to say, though you're probably not enjoying it," Candace said, chuckling, "but I hope you understand it."

"Sure." *No.*

"Sadie," Justin said, "this is my older brother, Bennett, and his fiancée, Hannah Yates."

Bennett was tall and had on a suit that probably cost more than her car. Hannah, on the other hand, had short, spiky black hair and was wearing worn jeans, work boots and a T-shirt that read Yates Construction.

She liked Hannah already.

"Sorry," Hannah said, "but Ben snatched me up off a jobsite and didn't give me a chance to change."

"Why should you change?" Bennett asked. "You look gorgeous. As always."

Candace ignored the two of them giving each other moony looks and concentrated on Justin instead. "Can I hold him?"

"Sure, Mom." Justin handed the tiny boy over to his mother.

"He's not very good with strangers," Sadie said quickly and then watched as her son proved her a liar. The tiny boy looked at Candace, then reached up to tug her hair as he babbled incoherently.

"Oh, yes, you are your daddy's son, aren't you?" She glanced first at Sadie to say, "He's just adorable." And before Sadie could say anything, Candace looked at her youngest son. "He has your dimple."

"Okay," Bennett announced, "if we're down to discussing my brother's dimples, I'm out. You guys do the baby thing while Justin shows me the hotel."

Sadie gave Justin a don't-you-leave-me-here-alone glare, but he only shrugged and walked off with his brother. For a long moment, she considered snatching up her baby and running, just to escape.

Instead, she plastered a smile she didn't feel onto her face and decided to stand her ground. For now.

"I can imagine you're not thrilled that I dropped in on you," Candace said, still smiling and cooing at Ethan.

"No, I… Well." She took a breath, then blew it out. "No."

Hannah laughed at that. "Know just how you feel. She 'dropped in' on me once, too. At a jobsite. She wanted to give me a talking to and explain what was wrong with Ben. I didn't like it, but that worked out okay."

"Oh, sweetie," Candace said, "it only worked because you loved Bennett. And," she added, with a considering look at Sadie, "I have the feeling that Sadie loves my Justin…"

Thankfully, Ethan chose just that moment to start fussing. Sadie used that excuse to say, "I'm really sorry but he needs to eat and—"

"Could I do it?" Candace asked. "It's been a long time since my granddaughter was this small, and I do miss babies."

Sadie looked at the older woman, really looked at her, and for the first time, saw beyond the elegance to the nice woman with kind eyes. Going with her instincts, Sadie said, "Sure. Let's go over here. His bottle's in the bag."

"Oh, isn't this fun?" Candace gave Hannah a nudge. "You'll have to give me one of these soon."

"We're working on it," Hannah assured her with a grin. "Every chance we get."

"Well, as I told Bennett not too long ago, a healthy sex life is important to any good relationship."

Surprised, Sadie stared at her for a second, then noticed Hannah shrugging. Justin's family was a little different than how she'd imagined them. She'd just assumed they'd be rich and snooty and too high-brow for her. So far, not so much.

Once Candace had the bottle, she laid Ethan back in her arms, smiled down at him and held that bottle while his little hands batted at hers. "Oh, Sadie, I'm so happy to meet my beautiful grandson. I hope you'll forgive me for just crashing in on you."

"Sure." That was knee-jerk polite, so she added,

"Of course. I do understand. My mom would have done the same thing."

"Oh, I think your mother and I will get along famously."

"I doubt we have to worry about that," Sadie said. "Justin and I aren't together."

"Oh, I wouldn't give up just yet," Candace said.

The sea breeze tossed the leaves of the tree, sending dappled shade dancing across their faces. The mingled scents of the flowers gathered on the courtyard were almost overpowering. Surrounded by beauty, Sadie tried to enjoy the women talking with her.

"The second reason I wanted to come," Candace said quietly, "was because I wanted to meet the woman who has my youngest son all twisted up."

Sadie laughed. Looking from Candace to a sympathetic Hannah and back again, she said, "Oh, no, I don't."

Candace shook her head and said, "I know my kids, Sadie. Justin has never been so protective. Not just of the baby but of you. He didn't tell us about you, you know."

"Because he didn't think I was important enough to mention."

"Oh, just the opposite, dear." Candace freed one hand long enough to pat Sadie's. "If you weren't important to him, he'd have told us everything. But because you are, he held back. Keeping you private. For himself. It's very Justin of him.

"Just as it was very Bennett to make an idiot of himself with Hannah. Isn't that right?"

Hannah sighed and grinned. "Have to say, she does know her children."

"That's why I wanted you to meet Hannah," Candace said. "She's marrying a Carey man, so she can really commiserate with you if you need it."

"And you will," Hannah said with a nod. She propped her elbows on the table and said, "I love Ben to pieces. But even now, he drives me crazy sometimes. He's opinionated and stubborn and sweet and loving. I have to say, the Carey men are kind of weird, but generally, they're worth the trouble."

"There." Candace beamed at Hannah before telling Sadie, "You see?"

"Look," Sadie said, "I appreciate the solidarity and the advice and even the sympathy. But I'm not the problem. I do love him. But that will pass. Eventually."

Hannah and Candace exchanged a long, telling look.

Sadie sighed. "You don't understand. Justin proposed, but made it more of a business deal. He doesn't want love involved. Just teamwork."

"What did I tell you," Hannah muttered. "Weird."

"Weird or not," Sadie continued, "I'm not going

to live my life that way. So there really isn't anything you guys can do."

Candace sighed. "It's very disappointing to hear that I have another son who is being shortsighted. Although," she added, "their father hasn't been much better lately."

"Look," Sadie said. "I really do appreciate all of this, but Justin and I aren't together and we're not going to be."

"You have a child together. Ethan is a Carey."

Sadie felt a quick jolt of panic at Candace's quiet words. Was that a warning? A threat?

"That means you and Justin will always be linked together," the older woman said. "And no one can read the future, Sadie." She smiled down at the baby. "He's all finished. Aren't you, my darling?" Lifting him onto her shoulder, she patted his back until he burped, then she gave him a proud smile.

"Babies change everything, Sadie. You'll see."

"Thanks, Candace," she said, "but I don't want to be married because of a baby any more than I want to be just a business deal."

"And I don't blame you a bit," Candace said, and reached out to pat Sadie's hand. "Oh, honey. Patience is a must when dealing with a Carey male."

"She's not wrong," Hannah mused.

"What do you think they're talking about?" Justin shot a look out the windows at the women.

"Us, of course," Bennett said, strolling through the hotel, checking everything with quick eyes that never missed a thing. "What do women always talk about? The men in their lives and how to fix them."

Justin glared at his brother's retreating back. "I don't need fixing."

"Yeah, neither did I," Bennett said, turning to wink at Justin. "But I do enjoy having Hannah try."

"I should go out there."

"Are you worried?"

"Sadie doesn't trust the Careys."

"Neither did Hannah."

Justin sighed and pushed one hand through his hair. "How'd you change her mind?"

"By loving her. By letting myself love her."

Justin shoved his hands into his pockets. Love. It kept coming back to that one, small word. One emotion that so many people had tried and failed to define. What he felt for Sadie was stronger than anything he'd ever known. And could *probably* be described with that word she wanted to hear.

Well, he wanted to be with her. Wanted to give her what she needed. Wanted the partnership they'd built over the last few months, but that one little word kept stopping him because once it was said, there was no going back.

And he still couldn't risk it.

"I've never said that word to a woman before, Bennett. And I can't say it to Sadie yet."

"Why the hell not?"

He scowled at his brother. "I've got too much to prove."

"To whom?"

"You. Dad. *Me*."

"You've already convinced me. Dad's got his own issues," Bennett pointed out, "and if *you* don't believe in you, who the hell will?"

"I've got a *son*, Bennett," Justin said, and even hearing the words aloud still felt strange to him. "I owe him something, too."

"Yeah, you do." Bennett stared at him. "You owe him a family if you can give him one. If you love Sadie, step up. Hell, Justin, I almost lost Hannah because I was too stupid to see the truth." Bennett slapped his brother's shoulder. "Be better than me."

Justin nodded as his brother's words resonated with him. He had been stupid. But he didn't have to stay that way. "I hate that you're right, Bennett. But I don't hate that you said all of that." He was risking what he had with Sadie because he was afraid to risk Sadie's heart. Suddenly, it made zero sense.

A year and a half ago, he'd left Sadie because she had become too important to him and he'd had too much to prove. Now he loved her. Yes, that word. He loved her. And he'd been willing to walk away again because he couldn't risk her happiness until he was sure he would succeed. How could he make promises to her when the promises to himself were unfulfilled?

But hadn't he proved it? Hadn't he done what he'd promised himself he was going to do? The Carey Cliffside was a reality and in two weeks, it would be open and he *knew* people would flock to this amazing spa hotel at the ocean's door. He'd done it. The only thing he had left to prove was to Sadie. He had to prove to her that he loved her. That he would never leave her again.

Otherwise, how many hotels would it take for him before he could consider himself a success? Before he could offer Sadie what she deserved?

"I want Sadie with me," he said, nodding to himself, shooting a glance at his brother. "I want to be a permanent part of my son's life."

"Glad to hear it," Bennett said. "Because you two did a hell of a job on this hotel/spa—and we're going to need Sadie for the Newport Beach hotel."

Justin laughed out loud. "Leave it to you to talk business while I'm having an epiphany." Shaking his head, he let Bennett talk business while his own mind shot straight to Sadie. He had a lot he wanted to talk to her about. Once Sam's wedding was over, once the hotel was opened, he would give her all the romance she needed.

He wanted to build a family with the woman he loved. But could he do it? Could he convince her to trust him? To trust his family? He had to make a phone call. Get the wheels moving. So he could show Sadie he meant what he said. "I've got to call Jackson."

"The family lawyer? Why?"

"Because, Bennett…" Justin grinned at him. "I'm going to be better than you."

"Hah!" Bennett slapped his back. "Only this once, Justin."

"Thanks. For coming down here. For telling me what I needed to hear."

Bennett smiled. "Women will mess a man up, Justin." He sighed. "But I'm here to tell you, it's worth it. Hannah is…*everything* to me. Make the right moves, Justin. You won't regret it."

Justin thought about it. Thought about the last week, when he and Sadie were so close and yet miles apart. Thought about the long, empty nights without her. And he knew. He was willing, finally, to take the biggest risk of his life.

He hoped it wasn't too late.

Ten

An hour later, Bennett stepped out of the hotel, walked straight to his fiancée and kissed her. Then he looked at Sadie. "It's a great place, Sadie. I think we're going to do really well together."

She knew about Bennett and the Carey Corporation investing in the Carey Spa Hotel group and she was all for it. One thing she could give the Careys. They were very successful in business. If they could continue the partnership through other hotels, she would be making sure that Ethan's future was safe.

"I'm glad you like it," she said, and watched Candace swaying in place to keep a now sleeping Ethan happy. Did the little boy know somehow that it was his grandmother holding him? That sounded fanciful, she knew, but Ethan had really connected with Candace right away.

The Carey family showing up unannounced had worried her, but they were so nice. So…normal, that Sadie was relaxing and trying to remember why she'd been leery in the first place.

"Oh, I more than like it." He looked at Hannah and said, "We're going to put a bid in on the Newport Beach hotel in a couple weeks and *you*, my gorgeous contractor, are going to be running the remodel."

Hannah grinned at him. "I'll try to work you in. I've got to finish the castle at Jack's house first."

"Please. That's almost done." Bennett kissed her again. "Work me into your schedule. You're the only contractor I trust to do the job."

"Sweet-talker," Hannah said with a smile.

"Where's Justin?" Sadie asked, looking toward the hotel. He'd taken Bennett on a tour—why hadn't he come out with his brother?

"Oh," Bennett said, dropping one arm around Hannah, "he's making a phone call. Wanted to talk to Jackson."

Sadie smiled. "Who's Jackson? Another brother?"

"Oh, no," Candace said as she kissed Ethan's forehead. "Jackson is the family lawyer." She didn't notice when Sadie went completely still.

Swallowing hard, Sadie asked, "Why did he have to call a lawyer?"

"No idea," Bennett said, oblivious to Sadie's distress. "Mom, I know you're having a great time, but we need to head back before the traffic is more of a nightmare than usual."

Sadie heard them, like buzzing noises inside her head. Fear thrummed through her bloodstream with every beat of her heart. But she didn't let it show. Couldn't. She knew it was important to smile and nod, and when Candace handed Ethan to her, Sadie cuddled him close, steadying herself by inhaling the soft, sweet scent of him.

"Fine," Candace said. "We'll go. But we'll be back for the wedding, Sadie, so we'll see you in a week, yes? And oh, wait until Martin sees his grandson."

"You care what Dad thinks?" Bennett asked.

"Don't be ridiculous, Bennett," Candace said. "I love your father very much."

"Right. That's why you're living with me."

"Us," Hannah corrected.

"Well, with any luck, I may be moving out of your house soon. I believe Martin may be coming around," Candace said with a tiny smile of satisfaction.

They were still talking, laughing, joking with each other. Sadie knew it, but she wasn't registering any of it. All she could think about was that Justin was calling the family lawyer. Why? Her stomach tightened and a knot of worry lodged in her throat. Somehow she smiled at Candace, said *something* to Bennett and Hannah and waved as they walked off.

Her mind racing, Sadie clung to Ethan. She wanted to take him and run. Lawyers? This could only mean one thing. Justin had been playing her all along. She'd begun to trust him and he'd simply been setting her up. That was why his family had come here today. To see Ethan. To make sure he was Carey-worthy before they took him from her.

Was she being paranoid? Or were all her fears suddenly springing into life? Sadie couldn't risk it.

"Oh my God, Ethan," she whispered, looking around as if she expected someone to leap out from behind the arbor to snatch her son from her arms. "We have to get out of here."

Panic rushed through her, stealing her breath, stinging her eyes with tears of betrayal. How could he do this to her?

"It's because I said no to his lame proposal," she whispered, stunned as the realization slapped at her. "Of course. He gave me a chance to keep my son. All I had to do was marry a man who didn't love me."

He'd called the Carey family lawyer to get a custody suit rolling. She knew it. Just as she knew she'd never be able to win in court against the Carey money. The Carey family reputation. So she wouldn't fight. She'd run.

A year and a half ago, Justin had walked out on her, leaving her broken. This time she would be the one walking.

"Hey," Justin called as he strolled out of the hotel. "Did they leave?"

"Yes," she said, and forced a smile that felt tight on her face. "They wanted to beat the traffic. What were you doing?" Would he lie? Would he be honest and tell her what he was up to?

"Oh," He shrugged. "I put a call into a Realtor I know in Orange County. Bennett and I want to move on the Newport Beach property right after the grand opening here."

Lies. He had looked her in the eye and lied. She swallowed back the pain, the humiliation, and said, "That sounds great. But for right now, Ethan's sleeping so soundly I'm going to take him up to our room, put him to bed."

"I'll do it," he said, stepping forward to reach for his son.

It was all she could do not to turn and run. Instead, her arms tightened instinctively around Ethan and the little boy stirred fretfully. "It's fine. I've got him. You should, uh, talk to Sam. Make sure we're on schedule for the wedding and the opening."

He frowned a little as he watched her, so she smiled again to ease his mind. "Okay. I will," he said. "We're running out of time, aren't we?"

"What?" Another spurt of panic.

"To get everything set for the wedding." He frowned again. "Are you okay?"

"Fine," she said sharply. "Just tired."

"Maybe you should lie down with Ethan."

"Not a bad idea," she agreed. "We'll see you in a couple of hours, then."

"Okay."

She turned to walk into the hotel and only paused when Justin called, "Sadie?"

Looking over her shoulder at him, she waited.

"When the wedding and the opening are over, we have to sit down together and talk about something."

A lead ball dropped into the pit of her stomach, but she didn't let him see it. Sadie knew what he wanted to talk to her about. But she wouldn't be here to listen.

Nodding, she walked into the hotel, forcing herself to take slow, steady steps.

Justin hadn't seen Sadie in hours. But he was giving her some space because of his family's surprise visit. Talking to Bennett had helped Justin out a lot. But he'd seen the look on Sadie's face when they'd all arrived. When his mother had been holding Ethan.

Fear. She didn't trust him, he thought, and then considered it. Why would she? She didn't trust his family and again, why would she? Hopefully, after she heard what he'd talked to the lawyer about, that trust would come. Looking back now, he could see that his suggestion to get married because they made a great team at work had been the biggest mistake he'd ever made.

Justin could admit that he'd been stupid about that. But he'd been too scared to admit he was in love. Real love. Hell, that was a big admission for any man. Now he knew that the only way Sadie would ever believe that he loved her was if he gave her a real proposal. A real promise. And he was ready to do that now.

He walked into the lobby of the Cliffside and paused to take a look around. Cleaning staff was busy, polishing floors, dusting, setting out vases of flowers on the gleaming wood tables. Two women stood behind the reception desk, answering phones.

Apparently, all of the advertising was doing the job, because they were taking reservations now for the opening of the hotel. He walked over, waited for one of the women to hang up, then asked, "How's it going?"

"It's amazing, Mr. Carey," she said with a wide grin on her face. "We're almost booked out. Only a few rooms left and the treatment rooms are booked solid for the first week."

"Just what I wanted to hear," he said, then left when the phone rang and she answered, "Carey Cliffside."

It sounded good. Sounded perfect. Maybe he

didn't have to wait for the wedding and the opening to be over. Maybe the time for a real proposal
was at the precipice of their new beginning. After
all, he wanted Sadie to know that win or lose with
the hotel, he wanted to be with her. He was finished
waiting, planning. Now was the time to act.

But even as he thought about going upstairs to
propose, he realized he didn't have a damn ring.

"Can't propose without a ring," he muttered, and
turned on his heel. Smiling, he left the hotel, headed
for the best jewelry store in town.

It took Sadie a little over three hours to drive to
her parents' house in Bullhead City, Arizona. Their
house was brand-new and in an adults-only golf
course community. For herself, Sadie would miss
living right beside the ocean too much to make the
move. But she knew her parents were loving the
change.

She parked in front of their house and winced
when she got out of the car. It was only June and
already the heat was blistering. She glanced up at
the brassy sky and smiled sadly at the two small
clouds drifting lazily across it. Her parents' house
was one-story, sitting on a knoll so that there was a
view of the Colorado River in the distance. Desert
landscaping surrounded the house, but there were
two trees in the yard that would, one day, provide
shade. While she stood there staring, the front door

flew open and her mother ran down the walkway toward her.

"Sadie! What a wonderful surprise!" Monica Harris was tall, like her daughter, with chin-length, dark brown hair cut into a bob that suited her perfectly. She was slim and tanned and the white shorts and dark green shirt she wore looked great on her. "Hi, Mom." Tears stung her eyes as her mother wrapped her in a tight hug. This was what she'd needed. After a long minute, she said, "Yeah, I just had to get out of San Diego for a while."

Monica held on to her daughter's shoulders and pulled back, studying Sadie's face. "Something's wrong. So you come in and you tell me about it."

Sadie glanced at the house. "Where's Dad?"

Monica was opening the back door to get at her grandson. "Oh, he's golfing with his buddies. If he doesn't get heatstroke, he should be home in an hour."

"Okay…" Good. It would give her a chance to talk to her mom first.

"There's my boy!" Monica scooped him up out of the car seat. Ethan laughed and kicked, happy to be out.

Then, Monica spotted Sadie's suitcase and asked, "How long are you staying?"

"I don't know yet, Mom." Sadie took a breath, looked at her son, then met her mother's gaze. "I don't know anything."

Sympathy shone in her mother's eyes and Sadie's aching heart eased just a little. "Oh, sweetie, come on inside. You can tell me everything over a slice of cake."

"Chocolate?" Sadie asked with a smile.

"Is there any other kind?"

She'd needed this, Sadie thought. Her mom's steadiness—not to mention her cake. And to be here with people who loved her and understood her and, most important, the two people in the world who would support her, no matter what.

"You just disappeared with the man's *child*?"

Sadie sighed in the face of her father's outrage. If this was support, she wasn't loving it.

"Really?" Sadie asked. "Mom laid into me already and the minute you get home, you do the same?"

"Baby girl," her father said, moving in close enough to give her a hard, fast hug. "You can't take a man's child away. Hell, you can't take *anyone's* child away. It's not right. You're worried that's what he's going to do to you? But you just did it, to *him*."

God, he was right. In her defense, she hadn't been thinking. Sadie had been running on pure emotion.

"You're gonna scare the crap out of the man, too." Her father studied her closely. "Is that what you wanted?"

"Of course not," Sadie said, a little insulted that

he would think so. "I just had to get Ethan out of there. Justin was talking to their family lawyer."

"That could have been about anything," her mother added while she bounced Ethan on her lap.

"No." Sadie had been thinking about this for hours and she knew she was right. He'd called the lawyer right after his mother and brother had seen Ethan. The Careys wanted her little boy and they couldn't have him.

She picked up her glass of iced tea and took a drink. "I can't believe I came to you guys and you're on Justin's side. What happened to unconditional support?"

Max Harris laughed shortly. "We're always on your side, Sadie. We love you. That doesn't mean we won't tell you when we think you're wrong."

"And you're wrong this time, sweetie," her mom said.

"No, I'm not." Sadie's gaze shifted to her son and everything in her told her that she'd done the right thing to protect him. The *only* thing she could have done.

Her mother smoothed Ethan's silky hair back from his forehead and a soft smile curved her mouth as she shook her head. "Imagine what Justin's going to think, *feel* when he finds out you two are gone."

"He'll be furious when he finds out that Ethan is gone," she acknowledged. "But he won't care about me," Sadie said, shaking her head. She really hated saying that out loud. Heck, she hated to admit it to herself at all. But the simple truth was, Justin didn't love her. He only wanted her because of their son. Hadn't he already offered her the least romantic proposal in history? And the kind of marriage he was interested in was so...lonely.

"Well, if that's true," her father said with a hard hug, "then the man's a fool."

She went up on her toes to kiss her dad's cheek. Sadie hated bringing trouble here. Her parents had a new, more relaxing life and her father hadn't looked this good in years. "I shouldn't have come and dragged you guys into this."

"Who else would you drag?" her father demanded, making her smile. "You always come to us, kiddo. We might not always think you're right, but we'll always love you. And Ethan."

"I know that," she said, leaning into his hug. He smelled like peppermint and sunblock and made her feel safe. "And I'll call Justin. I don't want him to be scared for Ethan."

"Or for you."

"Dad, I told you. He only proposed because he said we made a good team. Because we share Ethan." One tear escaped her eye and she swiped it away impatiently.

"Honey..."

"No." She turned and looked at her mom before

shifting her gaze to the happy baby holding his own hands. "I have Ethan. And you and Dad. I'll be fine."

She'd turned her phone off when she left San Diego, so when she slipped outside and turned it back on and it lit up with a dozen texts and just as many voice mails, she wasn't surprised. She flipped through the texts quickly.

The same theme over and over. Where are you? Damn it, call me.

She didn't bother listening to the voice mails. What would be the point? Sadie paced around her parents' patio and dialed Justin.

"Where the hell are you?" he demanded, startling her. She hadn't even heard the phone ring.

"I'm at my folks' house. In Arizona."

"Arizona?" She heard anger and frustration and fear in his voice and she was sorry for the last. "Is everything all right? You and Ethan are okay?"

"Yes, of course."

"Good. How could you just leave? Without a word?"

"You did the same thing, remember?" Sadie countered, and let her own anger jump to the fore-front. "A year and a half ago, I told you I loved you and you left. Well, this time, it was my turn to disappear."

"Your turn?" The outrage in his voice made her wince. "That's what this is about?"

She closed her eyes and could just *see* him, pacing, pushing his hand through his hair, a death grip on his phone.

"No, Justin," she said and fought to speak past the pain thrumming in her chest. "I left because I had to. And I only called to let you know that Ethan is fine." She took a breath. "As for the hotel and our partnership, you can have it all. My twenty-five percent was a way for me to take care of Ethan's future. But that's pointless if I don't have him with me. So keep the hotel. I don't care. But you can't have my son."

"What are you talking about?"

"I'm staying in Arizona, Justin." She walked across the yard to stand under one of the young trees. "Ethan's safe and he's going to stay that way."

"Why wouldn't he stay safe? What the hell happened when you were talking to my family?"

"You know exactly what happened. Why else would you have called your family lawyer?"

"Is that what this is about? Because I called Jackson? For God's sake, Sadie—"

"Because you called a lawyer and then lied to me about it. I don't want to hear anymore lies," she said, cutting him off again. She couldn't hold back her tears for much longer, so she needed to get off the phone fast. Damned if she'd let him hear her cry. "I have to go. Ethan needs me."

Two hours later, Ethan parked his rental car outside the Harris house. When he turned the engine off, he just sat there for a minute or two, getting a grip on the fury that had ridden him all the way from California.

Sadie had walked away from him. Left him without a damn word and now he knew exactly how she'd felt when he'd done the same damn thing to her. He didn't like it a bit.

More than that, though, he knew he'd deserved this. Sadie had had every reason to take their son and leave. He hadn't given her any reason to trust him. To believe that now would be different from when they were together before. So she'd taken their son to protect him—from his father. And wasn't that a bitch?

It hadn't been hard to find her parents. A call to the Carey company had put three of Bennett's best employees on the task. One to find the Harris family, one to rent Justin a car and the third to get the Carey family jet ready. Which meant that by the time Justin left his car in short-term parking at the San Diego Airport—the Carey family jet was ready and waiting to take him to Bullhead City, Arizona.

Now he stepped out of his rental car, marched up the walk to the front door and rang the bell.

She opened the door and her eyes went wide.

"Surprise," he said and stepped forward. Pushing past her into the house, he walked into the great room, spotted his son on the lap of Sadie's mother and took his first easy breath in hours. Nodding at the older couple, he said, "Mr. and Mrs. Harris, I'm sorry to meet you this way, but I've got some things to say to your daughter."

"I'll bet you do," Max Harris mused.

"Mom, Dad, would you excuse us?" Sadie gave her parents a look that said, *Help me out here.*

"I don't think so," her mother said and sat back in the chair, cuddling Ethan close.

Sadie took a deep breath. "Fine. Why are you here, Justin?"

"You're kidding, right?" Justin walked in close to her, grabbed hold of her shoulders and forced her to look up at him. "You were *gone*. Ethan was *gone*. Then when I couldn't get hold of you—answer your damn phone from now on—the fear kept growing until I finally found out that you're here. With your parents. Then you tell me you're not coming back? I can have the hotel but not you? Not my son?"

"You don't have to repeat it all," she muttered, throwing an uncomfortable glance at her parents.

"Yeah I do. Just to believe it's real." His hands on her gentled and he asked, "Why, Sadie? Just tell me that much. Why?"

She lifted her gaze to his. "Because you called your lawyer. Because you're going to try to take Ethan from me."

Justin choked out a strangled laugh. "What are you talking about? Where did that even come from?"

He noted how interested Sadie's parents were.

Well, that couldn't be helped. He was finally going to say everything he wanted to say to Sadie and he didn't care if they had an audience.

"Right after your mother and brother came," she was saying, "right after they saw Ethan, you called your family lawyer. Why else would you do that?"

Justin felt her words land like a slap in the face. He'd kept her at such an emotional distance that she actually believed he would steal their son?

"I'm sorry, Sadie," he whispered and watched her eyes fill with tears.

"So it's true?" she asked quietly.

"No, it's not true. I'm sorry I was an ass for so damn long that you can't trust me. I never should have walked away from you, Sadie." He smoothed the pad of his thumb over her cheekbone, wiping away a single tear. "And you should have told me about Ethan."

"Yes, she should have," her father said.

Her mother added, "We told her to."

"Yes," she said, as she rolled her eyes. "Everyone is right. I should have told you, Justin. And…I'm sorry we're doing this with an audience."

"I don't care who hears me," Justin said, meeting her gaze. "As long as you do. Look, I know you don't trust me and I don't know how to change that except by showing you that you can. It might take years to prove it to you, but I'll put in the time because I love you, Sadie."

Her breath caught and she bit down on her bottom lip. She looked like she wanted to believe, but was again afraid to trust.

"The reason I called the lawyer was because I wanted to start adoption procedures. I want Ethan to have my last name. Hell, I want you to have it, too."

"What are you saying?" Sadie whispered.

"I'm saying I want you and Ethan to be my family."

"Oh, Justin…"

"Just wait a second," he blurted out, rubbing her shoulders, simply because he needed to feel her. To know she was there. With him. Where she belonged. "I'm finally saying it, Sadie. So just… Hear me out. Please. I'll work my ass off to prove myself to you. To show you how much I love you and Ethan. But the next time you're pissed at me, I'd appreciate it if you'd just tell me what's going on instead of running?"

She gave him a soft smile. "I will. I think maybe we've both done enough running from each other. Maybe it's time we ran *to* each other."

"Good idea," he said as his heart seemed to fill beyond what should have been possible.

"I never meant to keep Ethan from you, Justin." Sadie lifted one hand and cupped his cheek. Her touch filled all those empty, icy places inside him with warmth. "And you don't have to adopt your son because you're already listed on the birth certificate as Ethan's father."

"Thank you for that."

She smiled. "I couldn't take that from you or from Ethan."

"I do love you." He pulled her in close, wrapped his arms around her and gave her a quick, hard kiss. "We're going to make the best chain of spa hotels in the country. And we're going to do it together."

She smiled up at him and he loved seeing the sparkle back in those gold-flecked eyes. "Glad to hear it, since I own twenty-five percent of the business."

"No, you don't," he said and took her left hand in his. "From now on, it's fifty-fifty all the way." Holding her hand, he dropped to one knee and heard her mother gasp in delight. But all he could see was Sadie, watching him, her eyes glistening and that amazing mouth turning up into a smile.

Digging into his jacket pocket, he produced a square-cut, canary yellow diamond and held it at the tip of her ring finger. Waiting.

"Marry me, Sadie," he said. "Have more kids with me. Build a family, a legacy all our own. I swear I will love you forever. And if you ever feel like leaving again, you have to promise to take me with you."

"I think I can do that," she said, her smile wider, her eyes brighter.

"That's a yes?"

"Oh, yes, Justin. It was always yes."

He slid the ring onto her finger, then stood and swept her into a kiss that had their son clapping tiny hands and laughing. Sadie's parents cheered. And just like that, the rest of their lives started.

It was perfect.

Epilogue

Sam and Kate's wedding went off without a hitch. Even the weather cooperated, with a bright sun streaming out of a sky studded with white clouds. A gentle ocean breeze kept everyone from getting hot. The food was wonderful, the flowers glorious and the ceremony, brief and beautiful.

The best part of the day, though, for Sadie anyway, was the fact that she and Justin and Ethan were officially a family. She looked down at her gorgeous ring and saw more than a lovely stone. She saw the promise she'd longed for. Saw the love she'd dreamed of, and when Justin came up behind her and wrapped his arms around her, she leaned into his hold and smiled up at him, free now to love and be loved.

"It was great," he said. "The whole day. You and Kate really pulled it together."

Laughing, she said, "In spite of Kate's mom. It really was a wonderful day," she agreed, grinning up at him. "And you did a terrific job holding Sam together."

"It's pitiful," he said, shaking his head and smiling. "The man's nuts about Kate and nearly crumbled when he had to stand up in front of the crowd."

"Hmm. We'll see how you do when it's our turn."

He frowned a little and shivered. "Let's not think about that part yet."

Sadie laughed, hooked her arm through his and said, "We should probably get Ethan and give your parents a break from the baby."

"Yeah, good luck with that." Most everyone had gone, but there were a few people, obviously reluctant to leave, still swaying on the dance floor. Justin held on to Sadie's hand as he led her across the courtyard.

The Carey family sat around a large table and Sadie could smile now when she saw them all. The Careys were her family now. And the warmth she'd already received from them filled her heart. Justin's parents, Candace and Martin—with Martin holding Ethan and having what looked like an indepth conversation with the tiny boy. Justin's sister

Amanda sitting on her fiancé Henry's lap. His sister Serena's daughter, Alli, perched on her soon-to-be stepfather Jack's shoulders while Serena leaned into him. Bennett and Hannah holding hands on the table and watching Ethan with silly smiles on their faces.

As Justin and Sadie approached, Candace smiled warmly and said, "Perfect timing! We want to have a toast to all of the upcoming weddings in the family."

Justin sat down, and dragged Sadie onto his lap. Across the table, Ethan spotted them and laughed, chewing on his fingers. Sadie held Justin's hand and gave it a squeeze. She was just so happy she hardly knew what to do with herself. She had Justin. Ethan. Her own parents and now this wonderful family, too.

"Mom," Bennett said, gathering everyone's attention, "if we're going to toast to all of us, there's one more thing to be excited about." He looked at Hannah and she nodded.

"We didn't want to say anything, but what the hell, we'll risk it. Hannah's pregnant."

The whole table erupted in cheers, laughter and a few tears.

"Oh, this is so wonderful," Candace said. "Soon, I'll have two new sons and two new daughters." She glanced at her husband and smiled. "And just imagine all the grandbabies we'll have!"

Martin rose and drew Candace up to stand beside him. He held Ethan close to his chest, even when the baby began to chew on his two-hundred-dollar tie. Dropping his free arm around his wife's shoulders, Martin looked around the table, at each of his children and the partners they loved. "We'll toast to your weddings, to Bennett and Hannah's baby..."

Bennett kissed his fiancée soundly, making her laugh.

"And," Martin continued, "we'll toast to your mother and me and retirement."

They all groaned and Candace laughed and raised one hand. "No, it's real this time. Isn't it, Marty?"

He looked down at her and kissed her forehead. "It is. I'll never risk losing you again, Candy." Looking out at his family, he said, "Thanks to all of you falling in love, building your own futures, I finally realized that this time with Candy is the one thing I can't live without."

She laid her head on his chest and sighed, even when Ethan leaned forward to pat her face.

"We're taking a round-the-world cruise—we leave at the end of the week."

"I'm getting him out into the middle of the ocean, just to make sure that *this* time, retirement sticks," Candace said, giving her husband a nudge.

"It'll stick, Candy. I promise." Turning to their children again, Martin assured them, "We'll fly home for every wedding. And when the cruise is over, we'll be doting grandparents who take occasional trips."

Candace laughed happily and hugged Alli, when the girl came rushing up to her.

Martin lifted his glass and waited until everyone else had done the same. "The business is yours now. I trust you all to work together. Help each other. Love each other.

"And I know that the Carey Corporation, the Carey Center and the Carey legacy…are in very good hands."

* * * * *

*Don't miss the next Dynasties,
from Harlequin Desire!*

Dynasties: DNA Dilemma

*When a blueblood patriarch requests family DNA
tests for Christmas, he gets many more secrets
than he bargained for!*

Book one is available in February 2022

Secrets of a Bad Reputation
by Joss Wood

WE HOPE YOU ENJOYED
THIS BOOK FROM

✦ HARLEQUIN
DESIRE

*Luxury, scandal, desire—welcome to
the lives of the American elite.*

Be transported to the worlds of oil barons, family dynasties,
moguls and celebrities. Get ready for juicy plot twists,
delicious sensuality and intriguing scandal.

6 NEW BOOKS AVAILABLE EVERY MONTH!

#2851 RANCHER'S FORGOTTEN RIVAL

The Carsons of Lone Rock • by Maisey Yates

No one infuriates Juniper Sohappy more than ranch owner
Chance Carson. But when Juniper finds him injured and with amnesia
on her property, she must help. He believes he's her ranch hand, and
unexpected passion flares. But when the truth comes to light, will
everything fall apart?

#2852 FROM FEUDING TO FALLING

Texas Cattleman's Club: Fathers and Sons • by Jules Bennett

When Carson Wentworth wins the TCC presidency, tensions flare
between him and rival Lana Langley. But to end their familiy feud and
secure a fortune for the club, Carson needs her—as his fake fiancée. If
they can only ignore the heat between them...

#2853 A SONG OF SECRETS

Hana Trio • by Jayci Lee

After their breakup a decade ago, cellist Angie Han needs composer
Jonathan Shin's song to save her family's organization. Striking
an uneasy truce, they find their attraction still sizzles. But as their
connection grows, will past secrets ruin everything?

#2854 MIDNIGHT SON

Gambling Men • by Barbara Dunlop

Determined to protect his mentor, ruggedly handsome Alaskan
businessman Nathaniel Stone is suspicious of the woman claiming to
be his boss's long-lost daughter, Sophie Crush. He agrees to get close
to her to uncover her intentions, but he cannot ignore their undeniable
attraction...

#2855 MILLION-DOLLAR MIX-UP

The Dunn Brothers • by Jessica Lemmon

With her only client MIA, talent agent Kendall Squire travels to his twin's
luxe mountain cabin to ask him to fill in. But Max Dunn left Hollywood
behind. Now, as they're trapped by a blizzard, things unexpectedly heat
up. Has Kendall found her leading man?

#2856 THE PROBLEM WITH PLAYBOYS

Little Black Book of Secrets • by Karen Booth

Publicist Chloe Burnett is a fixer, and sports agent Parker Sullivan
needs her to take down a vicious gossip account. She never mixes
business with pleasure, but the playboy's hard to resist. When they find
themselves in the account's crosshairs, can their relationship survive?

**YOU CAN FIND MORE INFORMATION ON UPCOMING HARLEQUIN TITLES,
FREE EXCERPTS AND MORE AT HARLEQUIN.COM.**

HDCNM0122A

SPECIAL EXCERPT FROM

(H)HARLEQUIN

DESIRE

*Eve Martin has one goal—find her nephew's father—
and her unlikely ally is hotelier Rafael Wentworth, who's
just returned to Texas and the family who abandoned
him. Soon, she's falling hard for the playboy despite
their differences...and their secrets.*

Read on for a sneak peek at
The Rebel's Return, *by Nadine Gonzalez.*

"I'm opening a guesthouse in town, similar to this, but better."

"You're here to check out the competition, aren't you?"

Rafael raised a finger to his lips. "Shh."

"That's sneaky," Eve said with a little smile. "I knew you had a
motive for coming here."

He winked. "Just not the motive you thought."

She responded with a roll of the eyes. He noticed her long lashes
fanned the high slopes of her cheeks. In the intimate light of the inn's
lobby, her skin was smoother than he could have ever imagined.

Rafael was glad the tension that had built up in the car was
subsiding. He wanted to make her laugh again, the way she'd laughed
when they were alone in the garden. Her laughter had leaped out as
if springing from a sealed cave. He'd wanted to take her in his arms
and hold her close until she settled down.

"Incoming!"

Lost in the fantasy of holding her, he didn't quite understand
what she was saying. "What's that?"

"Just...shut up."

She stepped up to him and brushed her lips to his in a whisper of
a kiss. Rafael tensed, the muscles of his abdomen tightening. "Act
like you're into it," she murmured through clenched teeth. With
every nerve ending in his body setting off sparks, he didn't have to

rely on dormant acting skills. He gripped her waist, pulled her close and kissed her hard, deep and slow. She gripped the lapel of his suit jacket and opened to his kiss. He heard her groan just before she tore herself away.

"I think we're good," she said, her voice shaky.

He was shaken, too. "How the hell do you figure?"

"I kissed you to create a distraction," she said. "P&J just walked in."

Paul and Jennifer Carlton were the most annoying couple in Texas, but at this moment he was making plans to send them a fruit basket and a bottle of wine.

"Here I thought you wanted to test that 'sex in an inn' theory."

"Stop thinking that," she scolded. "They're right over there. Don't look now, though."

He wouldn't dream of it. Her swollen lips had his undivided attention.

"Okay… They've entered the dining hall. You can look now."

"Nah. I'll take your word for it."

The manager returned with the keys to their suite, the one with the two distinct and separate bedrooms. The man was a little red in the face from what he'd undoubtedly witnessed.

Rafael plucked the key cards from his hand. "I'll take those. Thanks."

"Anything else, sir?"

"Send up laundry services, will you?" Rafael said. "And your best bottle of tequila."

The manager cleared his throat. "Certainly, sir. Enjoy your evening."

Don't miss what happens next in
The Rebel's Return *by Nadine Gonzalez,*
the next book in the Texas Cattleman's Club:
Fathers and Sons series!

Available February 2022 wherever
Harlequin Desire books and ebooks are sold.

Harlequin.com

Get 4 FREE REWARDS!

We'll send you 2 FREE Books plus 2 FREE Mystery Gifts.

Harlequin Desire books transport you to the world of the American elite with juicy plot twists, delicious sensuality and intriguing scandal.

FREE Value Over **$20**

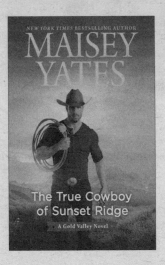